Life

Class

Life Class

Ann Charney

Cormorant Books

Canada Council for the Arts | Conseil des Arts du Canada

ONTARIO ARTS COUNCIL
CONSEIL DES ARTS DE L'ONTARIO
50 YEARS OF ONTARIO GOVERNMENT SUPPORT OF THE ARTS
50 ANS DE SOUTIEN DU GOUVERNEMENT DE L'ONTARIO AUX ARTS

Canadian Heritage | Patrimoine canadien
Canada

The publisher gratefully acknowledges the support of the Canada Council for the Arts and the Ontario Arts Council for its publishing program. We acknowledge the financial support of the Government of Canada through the Canada Book Fund (CBF) for our publishing activities, and the Government of Ontario through the Ontario Media Development Corporation, an agency of the Ontario Ministry of Culture, and the Ontario Book Publishing Tax Credit Program.

LIBRARY AND ARCHIVES CANADA CATALOGUING IN PUBLICATION

Charney, Ann, author
Life class / Ann Charney.

Issued in print and electronic formats.
ISBN 978-1-77086-296-8 (pbk.).— ISBN 978-1-77086-298-2 (mobi).—
ISBN 978-1-77086-297-5 (epub)

I. Title.

PS8555.H423L53 2013 C813'.54 C2013-903670-9
C2013-903671-7

Cover photo and design: Angel Guerra/Archetype
Text design: Tannice Goddard, Soul Oasis Networking
Printer: Friesens

Printed and bound in Canada.

MIX
Paper from responsible sources
FSC
www.fsc.org
FSC® C016245

The interior of this book is printed on 100% post-consumer waste recycled paper.

CORMORANT BOOKS INC.
10 ST. MARY STREET, SUITE 615, TORONTO, ONTARIO, M4Y 1P9
www.cormorantbooks.com

For Mel

PART ONE

Venice

I

The protégé

Helena is on her way to do a good deed. The pleasant glow of self-satisfaction that should rightfully be hers at this moment is fading with every step she takes. The interference comes from a throbbing in her ankle — the result of tripping over a rough patch of pavement in her Venice neighbourhood. The accident has persuaded Helena that her feet can no longer be trusted to navigate on their own; she must keep her eyes fixed on the ground when venturing outside.

She doesn't mind missing the sights along the way. After fifty years of life in Venice, the city's old stones and waterways are as familiar to her as her own body — and less changeable. The human landscape, however, still holds her attention, particularly the growing number of immigrants in the city — illegals for the most part, according to the papers.

Helena was once an immigrant herself — a young woman fleeing a country in ruins — but her interest in the new arrivals is strictly pragmatic. Human resource recruitment is how she sees it.

The business card she hands out to people she meets describes her as Canada's honorary cultural consul in Venice. To promote her other, more lucrative sidelines, she relies on word of mouth. Helena's talent for ferreting out people with useful skills, no matter how humble, is much in demand in her circle of acquaintances. In a difficult city like Venice, where everyone and everything moves on foot or by boat, sometimes a strong back is all it takes to save the day.

The young Africans selling knockoffs of Prada and Gucci bags along the bridges and squares of the main tourist thoroughfares look able-bodied, but she has written them off. Too specialized and too transient, appearing and disappearing each day as fitfully as the pigeons in Piazza San Marco. The same goes for the Gypsies who troll the tourist crowds in search of fresh pickings.

Helena has had better luck with recent arrivals from Eastern and Central Europe — a more dependable and ambitious lot. Right now she is on her way to meet Nerina, a young woman from the former Republic of Yugoslavia, whose life she is about to change for the better.

Helena spotted her latest protégé at the hairdressing establishment she frequents, Lorenzo's Istituto di Bellezza. Watching Nerina sweep hair cuttings into neat mounds — the movement of her arms graceful and arc-like, as if she were rowing a boat on calm waters — Helena felt there was more to the girl than met the eye.

The impression persists, even though Nerina has given her little to work with. Attempts to find out what lies behind the pretty face have been politely, but firmly, rebuffed. "Not important," she says when pressed for details.

Helena's offer of Italian lessons meets with an equally cool response. Despite her limited vocabulary, Nerina manages to make it clear that she is only biding her time in Italy until she can find a way to enter the US. "In America everyone speak English, no?"

Nerina spends much of her spare time watching US TV programs dubbed in Italian. This is not a frivolous pastime, she explains to Helena; it's her way of picking up useful clues about her next destination — how people live, what they eat, how they dress.

Now, thanks to Helena, Nerina will have an opportunity to pursue her research first hand. As she nears Lorenzo's on the Corso XXII Marzo, Helena smiles, anticipating Nerina's reaction.

Lorenzo greets Helena with an inquiring look. She doesn't have an appointment, and she can see all the chairs are taken.

"I've come to have a word with Nerina," she tells him. "Can you spare her for a few minutes?"

"*Prego, Signora, prego,*" he answers with a flourish of the hand, pointing to the back room. Helena thanks him and walks towards it.

Helena used to enjoy her weekly sessions in Lorenzo's chair, relaxing under a steady flow of flattery and gossip while he tended to her hair. That pleasure soured once she learned from Nerina how badly Lorenzo treats his foreign employees: paying them next to nothing, threatening disclosure to the police to keep them in line.

Thankfully, Nerina won't have to put up with Lorenzo much longer. "Come along," Helena says, taking hold of her hand and forcing her to abandon the pile of white robes waiting to be folded.

"I'll have her back in no time," Helena tells Lorenzo as they march past him. This time, his response is only a curt "*va bene.*"

"Not good time for break," Nerina says, following Helena into the café next door. "Lorenzo very busy."

"Relax," Helena tells her, sinking into her chair with relief. The pain in her ankle has become harder to ignore. "You don't have to worry about Lorenzo any more. I've found you a much better position with an American couple. Yes, real Americans, and rich to boot. They're looking for someone to help around the house and run errands. I convinced them to take you on."

Nerina presses her hands to her mouth in a gesture of astonishment. For a moment, her dark blue eyes are as bright as a child's with excitement, which soon gives way to a look of wariness.

"You tell truth about me?"

Helena knows Nerina is referring to her legal problems. As a citizen of Croatia, a country that is not a member of the European Union, she is obligated to seek permission to live and work in Italy. Nerina hasn't bothered to apply — the wait can be long and the outcome uncertain — preferring to focus her energies on finding a way to get to America. In the meantime, she does her best to stay under the radar of Italian authorities.

"Of course I told them. They don't care about your lack of papers."

The Ohstroms, Helena goes on to explain, are conscientious people, known for their support of worthy causes and their generosity towards those less fortunate. If anything, Nerina's illegal status is an asset.

"Your troubles are over. I promise," she says, patting the girl's hand.

Nerina still looks sceptical. Helena understands. Life has given her little reason to trust in promises.

She offers another bit of information, knowing it will appeal to Nerina. The Ohstroms are in the habit of going back and forth between Venice and New York. This means that Nerina will often have the house to herself, and, if she plays her cards right, they might take her along on one of their trips to New York.

The tantalizing possibility does the trick. "Helena, you best friend in the world," Nerina says, jumping up to hug the older woman.

"Stop that, and pay attention," Helena says, quickly disengaging herself from the girl's embrace. "They're expecting you tomorrow morning at nine o'clock. Make sure you're on time. Please listen carefully to their instructions and remember to keep your emotions in check. I don't want to have any reason to regret recommending you. One more thing: remember to smile a lot. Americans like people who look cheerful."

In compliance with Helena's advice, Nerina immediately responds with a wide smile, managing to make it look genuine.

Despite her show of sternness, Helena is pleased by Nerina's grateful response. The truth is it took some persuasion to convince the Ohstroms to take her on. They were looking for a local woman with whom they could practise their Italian.

But when it's time for her to leave, and Nerina rushes over to help her out of her chair, Helena responds with indignation. "If I want your assistance, I'll ask for it," she says, pushing the girl away.

She regrets her impatience as soon as she leaves Nerina, but knows she will give way to it again. She can't help it. The desperation she senses in the young woman — even though Nerina does her best to camouflage it — has that effect on her: reawakening memories that, so many years later, still unsettle her.

A moment later, Nerina rushes back out onto the street, looking distraught. But it's not Helena Nerina is worried about; it's Lorenzo.

"What if Lorenzo go to *Carabinieri* and make big trouble for me?" she asks.

"He won't. He knows he would be charged with hiring an illegal."

"*Vero*?" Nerina asks, using one of her few Italian words.

"Absolutely. You can put money on it."

Nerina repeats the unfamiliar expression to herself, smiling with pleasure. Forgetting about Lorenzo, she slips her arm through Helena's, ready to accompany her. Helena, however, has had enough of her changeable moods. "Go back," she says, pushing her away, more gently this time. She's no longer feeling irritable, just tired.

If she were really honest with herself, she thinks as she walks home, she would have to admit that her own moods are as changeable as Nerina's: vacillating between fondness for the girl and the need to protect herself from her. Now that she's freed Nerina from Lorenzo's tyrannical grip and found her a decent place to work, she intends to put some distance between them.

II

Christophe

Nerina does not discourage easily. Here she is on the landing outside Helena's door on a day when she has been warned that Helena is expecting visitors from Canada and does not wish to be disturbed.

"For you," she says, handing Helena the bouquet of sunflowers she's brought, which she presents with a mock curtsy. "Make room nice for guests."

Since Nerina started working for Bill and Alice Ohstrom, she has taken to dropping in at odd times of the day bearing gifts: flowers, persimmons, the occasional bottle of Prosecco. Helena has wondered if the offerings come out of the housekeeping allowance the Ohstroms give Nerina, but she doesn't really want to know. The Ohstroms, in any case, will never miss the money.

"You can't stay," she tells Nerina, ignoring the flowers. Her visitors won't be arriving for another two hours, but Helena needs the time to rest up for the work ahead of her — an exercise in charm and wit designed to ensure that her visitors speak well of her when they return home. Even at her advanced age, Helena must still hustle to survive.

"Ok, ok, I go," Nerina says unfazed, taking her time to arrange the flowers in a vase before she leaves.

When Helena lies down to rest, she finds her thoughts scurrying about like squirrels. To calm herself, she tries a little pre-emptive self-hypnosis: You will not, on any account, complain about the craziness of Italian politics; the incompetence of civil servants; the difficulties of growing old in a city with no elevators.

The talking-to seems to work. When the two Canadians arrive — a Montreal artist who goes by the single name of Christophe, and his girlfriend, Annette — they find their hostess in excellent humour, ready to entertain. Shuffling her vast repertoire of stories, Helena selects a succession of bright sketches that offer tantalizing glimpses of the rich life she's had and continues to have. Not only does she dazzle her guests, she also dazzles herself. Even the sore ankle feels better as she pops up and down every few minutes in search of props to accompany her stories: a gold-edged invitation to a gala on the royal yacht *Britannia*; a photograph of the Canadian ambassador and Helena in front of the Canada Pavilion at the Venice Biennale; a celebrated novel inscribed to her with gratitude by its author.

As the hours pass, the thought of dinner crosses Helena's mind. Apart from a steady flow of Martini & Rossi vermouth — a gift from a grateful client — she has nothing to offer her guests. Fortunately she can think of several Venetian homes, all better equipped than her own for the tiresome business of preparing food, and where she can always count on a warm reception. The welcome extends to any interesting guests she chooses to bring along, particularly now, in off-season, when the flow of visitors to the city slows to a trickle. But Helena is careful not to abuse her advantage in any season. Without missing a word of the conversation, she takes careful measure of her visitors to see if they will do.

Christophe and Annette look promising. They are attractive, reasonably intelligent and wonderfully responsive to the tired claims of Venice the beautiful. She will try them out on the Ohstroms, she decides; they are always interested in meeting new artists. The visit will also give her a chance to check on the restorations of the Ohstroms' house, which Helena found for them. Finding interesting dwellings for wealthy foreigners is another of Helena's sidelines.

"Sounds marvellous," Christophe says as soon as he hears Helena's plan. "I'd love to see the inside of one those old houses I've been admiring since we arrived. There's an air of mystery about them that makes you wonder what lies behind the façade."

Annette is less enthusiastic. "I think I'll head back to the hotel," she says. "I'm still pretty jet-lagged."

"Don't be silly. You can sleep in tomorrow," Helena hears Christophe say while she steps out of the room to collect her things. When she returns, she is relieved to find that Christophe's efforts of persuasion have failed. It's always easier to work with artists when their companions are not around.

The Ohstroms' small palazzo on Campo San Polo is only a few vaporetto stops from Helena's place. As the boat heads down the Grand Canal, Christophe's excited response to the illuminated monuments gliding past them makes Helena wish the trip were longer. It would be nice to find out that he has some talent to go along with the charm and the good looks. But lack of talent, she knows, is not necessarily a deal breaker on the road to success.

When they enter the campo they run into Nerina, who's just leaving the Ohstroms' house. She appears agitated and in a great rush to get away — nothing like the playful young woman bearing flowers of a few hours earlier.

"Everything all right?" Helena asks, but Nerina only nods and flies past her. Halfway across the campo, she turns back and shouts, "*Domani*." Helena ascribes her use of the Italian word to the presence of a stranger. But Nerina didn't really give her a chance to introduce Christophe.

"I can see Venetian women are as beautiful as I've heard," he says, watching Nerina beat her swift retreat.

Helena understands Christophe's mistake. Nerina may have no interest in learning Italian, but she's been quick to imitate local fashions. Dressed in Alice Ohstrom's expensive cast-offs, the ends of her long hair streaked in a clown's palette of pink, orange and red, Nerina looks like any of the stylish Venetian women she sees at gallery openings.

"How's Nerina doing?" Helena asks, finding herself alone with Alice while Bill takes Christophe on a tour of the house. She's hoping Alice can explain Nerina's abrupt departure.

"Fine, as far as I know. I've been out of the house all day. By the way, did I tell you Bill's bought a boat for exercise? He's trying to learn to row Venetian style — standing upright in the boat. Not as easy as it looks, according to Bill."

"About Nerina," Helena says, unwilling to abandon the subject. "She seemed in an awful hurry when we ran into her just now."

"I'm not surprised. She's a real live wire, that girl. Popping in and out pretty much as she pleases. Don't get me wrong. We enjoy having her — when she's around, that is."

The return of Bill and Christophe deflects Helena's attention from Nerina. Hearing the men talking about the history of the house, which dates back to the fifteenth century, she feels duty-bound to join in. Italian architecture of that period — the great *quattrocento* — is one of her special interests. It doesn't hurt to remind people like the Ohstroms that she was trained for culture, not commerce. Or that civilizations are remembered not for their business people, or their bankers, but for their art.

"You've just made me realize that all the reading I did in preparation for this trip barely scratched the surface," Christophe says, when she pauses to catch her breath.

"We all feel that way around Helena," Bill tells him. "She knows Venice better than most Venetians. Consider yourself lucky to be taken under her wing."

Helena, worn out from the exertion of her performance, responds with a weak smile. Her memory is not what it used to be and names and dates don't come to her as easily as they once did. Fortunately, Bill and Alice have now turned their attention to Christophe and his upcoming exhibition, leaving her free to sit back and relax.

Listening to the animated conversation around her, Helena feels she's done her work for the day, and done it well. Perhaps too well, she thinks, when Alice starts to quiz Christophe on his opinion of other artists — a game Alice has been known to play for hours.

"My dears, it's time for me to leave you," Helena announces, rising from the table. "Please carry on without me. No need to end the evening on my account."

"I'll come with you," Christophe says, quick to join her, "I have to be at the gallery first thing tomorrow morning." Maybe he doesn't care for the quizzing any more than she does.

"How did I do?" he asks her once they're alone. "I feel like I just faced the Inquisition in there."

"Get used to it," she tells him. "It's the price of admission, like singing for your supper. In any case, as far as Alice and Bill are concerned, there are no wrong answers. What they enjoy is reacting to other people's opinions, the stronger the better."

"I can handle that," Christophe says. "It's all the talk about the exhibition that has me worried. I'm not even sure we can get it up before the opening."

He continues to voice his concerns during the ride back on the vaporetto, ignoring the scenery this time. "Nothing has gone right so far. The L–shaped space of the gallery, with its walls tilting inward, is a challenge. To make matters worse, the workmen assigned to help me only show up when they feel like it and then pay no attention to my instructions."

Helena listens patiently, although she's heard it all before from other artists. The best thing she can do is simply to allow Christophe to unburden himself.

"Sorry to dump on you like this," he says when they reach her house. "I guess I'm just suffering from a bad case of nerves. This may be my only shot at a show in Venice, and I want to make the most of it. You understand, don't you Helena?"

"Get some sleep," she tells him, thinking longingly of her own bed. "I'll be at the gallery tomorrow and every day after that, if necessary. Don't worry, we'll straighten things out in no time."

Back in her flat, she takes a moment to glance at the notes on the exhibition that Christophe has left for her. His main installation, titled *The Waiting Room*, appears to consist of a circle of plastic covered chairs arranged around a frosted glass cubicle, and a soundtrack of a woman's voice reciting a list of symptoms.

What do doctors' waiting rooms — places to be avoided in her opinion — have to do with art? And why should a young man like Christophe be preoccupied by illness? She gave up years ago looking for a connection between the work of conceptual artists like Christophe and the Italian masterpieces of the past that drew her to Italy as a young woman. Their promise of a luminous world beyond the post-war drabness of her native Poland gave her the courage to make the difficult journey. The ominous promise of *The Waiting Room* is best left unexplored.

Still, she will do what she can for Christophe. It's both her job and her inclination to do so. Helena's faith in art may have waned, but she still has a soft spot for artists.

III

The break-in

As Helena rushes about helping Christophe with his exhibition, she forgets about Nerina's failure to keep her promise. *Domani* has come and gone, and there's still no sign of her.

When the telephone rings one night, wrenching her from a deep and blissful slumber — her reward for all that exertion — she's in no mood to be polite.

"Sorry to wake you," Bill Ohstrom apologizes. "I realize this is no time to call, but we have a bit of an emergency on our hands, and we need to speak to Nerina. I was hoping you'd know how to get in touch with her."

"Why? What's happened?" She can think of no good reason for a call at this late hour.

"We've just returned from a short visit to Rome to find the place in total disarray. I'm pretty certain we had a break-in. Nerina was supposed to be looking after the place while we were away, but she wasn't here when we got back. I want to talk to her before calling the police."

"Surely you don't think she had anything to do with this?" Helena asks, fully awake now and indignant on Nerina's behalf. Too many crimes in Italy are being blamed on illegal immigrants these days. It's not like the Ohstroms to succumb to this sort of scapegoating, but you can never tell how people will react when their property is threatened.

"Of course not," Bill quickly replies. "We simply want to see if she can shed some light on what happened. And if she was here during the break-in, she might be hurt."

Bill sounds sincere, but Helena still feels the need to defend Nerina, even though she's not being accused of anything. "Nerina would never get mixed up with any kind of criminal activity. She's much too frightened of being deported to tangle with the police."

But even as she speaks, Helena is thinking how little she knows about Nerina. Not only is she close-mouthed about her early years, she is equally circumspect about the present. Helena has no idea where Nerina lives, or how to reach her when she is not at the Ohstroms. Nor do the Ohstroms, apparently. Her certainty about Nerina's innocence is based on nothing more than instinct — a fact she is reluctant to reveal to the people she convinced to employ her.

She tells Bill she's misplaced Nerina's telephone number and will call him as soon as she finds it. For once, being old works in her favour. Old people are always misplacing things.

"Don't bother," Ohstrom replies. "I'm afraid we can't wait any longer to call the police. They will want to see the place before we start straightening it out. I doubt we'll get much sleep tonight, as it is. It's hard to get past the knowledge that your home has been invaded by strangers — the one place where you're supposed to feel safe."

Helena murmurs words of sympathy, but she can't bring herself to feel sorry for the Ohstroms. Insurance will cover whatever they've lost, and in no time at all their lives will run smoothly as ever. That's the way things are for people like the Ohstroms — the lucky ones. She can't expect him to understand that flight is the only insurance available for people like Nerina. No wonder she didn't stick around to wait for the Ohstroms to return.

Unable to get back to sleep, Helena occupies herself by working on the press release the gallery will send out before Christophe's opening, now only days away. A knock on the door soon breaks her concentration. It's followed by Nerina's voice calling her name.

The stiffness in her joints tells her she's been at the typewriter longer than she thought. As she makes her way slowly to the front door, she hears Nerina continuing to call her name. By now, Helena thinks, everyone in the building must have heard her.

Nerina falls into her arms, weeping, as soon as the door opens. "Bad trouble, very bad trouble," she repeats between heaving sobs.

Helena forces her into a chair, and brings her a glass of vermouth to calm her. Nerina gulps it down in one shot. Helena refills the glass, and, when the sobbing starts to subside, asks Nerina to explain herself.

Nerina, never easy to understand, is nearly incoherent. Slowly, with much patience on Helena's part, and ample use of mime on Nerina's, a story begins to emerge.

As far as Helena can make out, Nerina's troubles began in the early afternoon with the doorbell ringing. Pressing the intercom button, she heard a man's voice saying he had a package for the Ohstroms. Nerina had signed for deliveries in the past, so she didn't hesitate to open the door. A young man entered, carrying a box and a clipboard. But instead of handing the box to her, he reached inside, pulled out a rope and attempted to tie her up.

Here Nerina grabs her scarf and ties it around her hands to make her point.

"I scream loud," she says, demonstrating her vocal power before Helena can stop her. "So my friend upstairs can hear me."

"Friend? What friend?" Helena asks, startled. "You mean there was someone in the house with you?"

Nerina nods and gives Helena an imploring look. "Big, empty house, very scary for me. I invite friend to come."

"Who is this friend? How do you know him?" She has never heard Nerina mention any friends until now.

"Marco. He refugee like me. We live in same apartment." Seeing the look on Helena's face, Nerina quickly explains that she shares an apartment with five other people. "Venice very expensive."

Helena wonders if Marco was the reason for Nerina's haste the last time they met, but she wants to hear the rest of the story.

Nerina explains, in her fashion, how she tried to fend off her attacker, hitting him with any object she could grab. But it was a losing battle. By the time Marco finally came to her aid — he was in the shower and hadn't heard her first cries for help — she was on the floor, with her hands and feet tied. Marco, managed to sneak up on the intruder from behind and overpower him, finally pushing him out the back door.

"Well done," Helena says, exhausted, as if she had taken part in the struggle herself. But there is more to come, she realizes, as Nerina starts to cry again.

"Come now, the worst is over. There's no need to be so upset."

"Worst not over." Nerina wails. "I break lots of things in house. Expensive things. Vase, clock, mirror…"

"That's enough," Helena says, fatigue driving out her last shred of compassion. "Tomorrow you will explain the situation to the Ohstroms. After all, you were only defending yourself and their home. They'll understand."

"I never go back there," Nerina says, jumping out of her chair. "They make me tell story to police. Police send me back to Croatia."

"I will speak to the Ohstroms tomorrow and persuade them to keep you out of this. Now go home and let me get some rest. And leave me a number where I can reach you."

There is no telephone in her flat, Nerina tells her. Helena decides to believe her. The wait for landlines can be long in Venice, and as far as she knows Nerina doesn't own a cell phone.

"I call you from café," Nerina promises. At the door, she throws her arms around Helena. "You so good to me, Helena, like an angel," she says. "You have much condolence."

"The word you want here is compassion, not condolence," Helena says, laughing.

"Compassion," Nerina repeats dutifully. "English better soon. I promise."

IV

The Missing Brooch

Helena sleeps late the next morning, until she is awakened again by a call from Bill Ohstrom.

"I was just going to call you," she says as soon as she hears his voice, feigning an alertness she doesn't feel. "Nerina came to see me last night. You and Alice will be interested to hear what she had to say."

"Great, the sooner the better. Come for lunch."

In the Ohstroms' dining room, Helena chooses a seat facing a garden tucked in behind an adjacent building. She hopes this secret oasis of greenery, hidden from the street, will have a calming effect on her frayed nerves.

Bill and Alice, on the other hand, seem remarkably relaxed, despite last night's ordeal. "Hey, we're New Yorkers," Alice says, as she refills her wine glass. "City crime is nothing new to us."

Helena is pleased they're taking the break-in with such equanimity. It bodes well for Nerina.

"How did you find Nerina?" Bill asks, while he concentrates on serving the omelette he's prepared for their lunch. "I hope she's all right."

"Of course she's all right," Alice cuts in. "Girls like Nerina know how to take care of themselves. Bill seems to think all beautiful young women are in need of his protection. That's how I got him to marry me, and all these years later he's still no wiser."

"To tell you the truth, Nerina was pretty shaken when she came to see me last night," Helena says, choosing her words carefully. She has decided to give the Ohstroms an edited version of Nerina's tearful tale, avoiding any mention of Marco. In this account of the break-in, Nerina puts up a fierce fight, leaving in its wake a path of destruction, until finally — and single-handedly — she succeeds in scaring off the intruder.

"Lucky for her he was just a skinny kid," Helena tacks on in the interest of credibility.

"What did I tell you?" Alice asks, a note of triumph in her voice. "That girl knows how to look after herself."

"That was very brave of her," Bill agrees. "But why didn't she wait until we got back to tell us herself what happened?"

"I guess she panicked," Helena says, appealing to their sense of sympathy for the underdog. "She knew you would call the police and she didn't want to be around when they came."

"I only wish she hadn't used my Etruscan pitcher as a weapon," Alice says, pointing to a collection of shiny, black pottery shards on the sideboard. "Apart from its historic value, the piece has great sentimental attachment for me. My parents bought it in Greece, on their honeymoon."

Helena tries to look concerned, but she thinks Alice should blame herself instead of Nerina. If the pitcher meant so much to her, she should have kept it in a safer place.

"Nerina feels terrible about the damages she caused," she assures Alice. "The poor girl couldn't stop crying last night, she was so afraid of your reaction. I tried to tell her that you would understand, but she refused to believe me."

"Of course we understand," Alice replies, rising to the bait. "We're not cold-hearted slave masters."

"All things considered, I think we got off pretty easy," Bill says as he clears the table. "No one was hurt, and thanks to Nerina's bravery and quick thinking, nothing was taken."

"That's not quite true, Bill," Alice says. "There is the missing diamond-and-sapphire brooch."

"I'm sure you've misplaced it," Bill says, his dismissive tone indicating they have already discussed the matter and are not in agreement. "Let's wait a couple of days and see if it turns up before we accuse anyone. It's not as if this kind of thing hasn't happened before. Remember the ring you thought you'd lost, and then found in one of your drawers?"

Alice drops the subject, looking chastened. When Bill says they will do their best to protect Nerina from the police, she is quick to voice her support. "We'll just pop her into a closet and hide her should the police ever return."

Before heading home, Helena decides to pass by Christophe's gallery in Cannaregio to see how he is getting on. Crossing the Campo del Ghetto Nuovo — site of the oldest ghetto in Europe, despite its name — Helena is struck by the irony of her choices:

fleeing her Jewish past only to end up in a city that perfected the practice of herding Jews into corrals and branding them with yellow insignia.

Inside the gallery, most of the work is in place and Christophe waits, eager to show her around. As they make their way through the gallery, he launches into the backstory of each piece they pass — how it began, the discoveries along the way, the references that guided him.

"Save it for the critics and the buyers," she interrupts. "There will be plenty of people to impress both at the opening and at the Ohstroms' party afterward."

The light is fading by the time she emerges from the gallery. The dark waters of the San Vio canal that runs alongside her street reflect the illuminated windows of the nearby buildings. She pauses for a moment, watching the blurred images dance on the smooth surface of the water while she gathers strength for the eighty-six-step climb to her flat.

When she finally reaches the top of the landing, she is surprised to find Nerina waiting for her. From the number of cigarette butts in her coffee cup, it looks as if she's been there a while.

"I have good news for you," Helena tells her as soon as they're inside the flat. "The Ohstroms want you back and they're going to help you stay clear of the police. As far as they know, you were alone in the house when the attack took place. But I'm not going to cover for you again. You must promise not to bring Marco, or any other friends, into the house unless you clear it with the Ohstroms first."

"Marco not my friend," Nerina says.

"What happened? That's not the impression I had yesterday." Nerina's English is improving daily, but she's still hard to follow at times.

"I find out he take something from the house. To make it look like robbery."

"Alice's diamond-and-sapphire brooch?"

Nerina nods, looking alarmed. "They know?"

"Don't worry. Bill Ohstrom has persuaded Alice that she's misplaced it. Lucky for you, she has a history of misplacing things, but there's no time to lose. You must get the brooch back from Marco and put it where Alice is likely to find it. If Marco gives you any trouble, tell him I will not hesitate to report him to the police."

It's an idle threat — going to the police would expose Nerina as well as Marco — but Nerina takes it seriously.

"No police," she pleads, taking hold of Helena's hand. "I promise I put it back tomorrow."

A couple of days pass with no news, and Helena calls the Ohstroms to see if Nerina has kept her promise.

"I meant to call you," Bill says, as soon as he hears her voice. "Nerina's back, and Alice's missing piece of jewellery has turned up as well. It was right under her nose, just as I suspected, attached to the lapel of her favourite jacket. I guess we're both becoming more forgetful than we care to admit."

"I'm glad to hear it. I was a little worried on both accounts."

"Sorry about that. I've been out hunting ducks in the Lagoon, and forgot about everything else. I tell you, Helena,

I never imagined there was still so much wildlife so close to Venice. Being out there, a short boat ride from all the hustle and bustle of the city, surrounded by the stillness of the water and the occasional splash of a diving cormorant, it's easy to forget the city even exists."

Helena finds it hard to see the attraction in getting up before dawn to spend hours sitting in a small, cramped boat, but she doesn't want to spoil Bill's pleasure. Before the conversation ends, she thanks him and Alice again for volunteering to hold a reception at their house in Christophe's honour.

"We're glad to do it," Bill says. "We have to go back to New York the following week to look after a family problem. No idea how long that will take. The party will be just the right send-off."

V

Christophe's opening

The morning of Christophe's opening Helena awakes to the familiar wail of sirens, warning the city's inhabitants of rising water levels — *acqua alta*. Helena knows what awaits her. High tides and days of steady rain have once again turned the city's streets and squares into waterways. Looking out the window, she can see water lapping the front stairs of her building.

The flooding worsens by the time she has to leave for the gallery. Dressed in rubber boots and rain cape, and carrying an umbrella that threatens to invert with every gust of wind, she slowly navigates her way across wooden planks, strategically placed where canals and sewers have overflowed their banks.

The gallery is already half full by the time she arrives. Splattering wetness as she removes her outer gear, Helena feels like a dog shaking dry after a soaking. The sight of Christophe holding court at the centre of an attentive group improves her humour. She's in no hurry to reach him, preferring to keep her ears open for any favourable comments she can pass on to him later. Artists need all the encouragement they can get.

There are lively discussions going on in various parts of the gallery. Evidently she's not the only one mystified by Christophe's shabby waiting room and its litany of illnesses. This is not necessarily a bad thing. An impenetrable work is as good as a blank canvas, allowing critics to be as creative as they like without interference from the work itself.

From the buzz around her, she can hear that the process of illumination is already underway, layers of meaning being slathered onto the work like icing on a cake. She pauses to listen to Theodora Grimani, a woman she's known for years.

"All art is really a form of *memento mori*, reminding us we must die. A doctor's waiting room can be seen as a contemporary version of one of the Stations of the Cross along the Via Dolorosa of life."

Despite legitimate claim to the title of Contessa, Theodora, like Helena, has to scramble to survive. Her specialties include the production of books on the treasures of Venice, and private tours for wealthy foreigners willing to pay for the privilege of being shown the city by a member of one of its aristocratic families.

The two women have forged a useful alliance over the years, exchanging information and sharing clients. It was Theodora who recommended Helena to the Ohstroms when they were looking for a place in Venice.

She is also one of the few people in Venice who knows that Helena's family name, before her brief, ill-fated marriage to

Alberto Mariani, was Goldfarb. Helena doesn't pretend not to be Jewish; she just sees no reason to advertise the fact. It's a matter of simple prudence, as far as she is concerned. Throughout history, from the time of the Pharaohs on, it was never an advantage to be identified as a Jew, and it isn't now, even if you live in Israel. Fortunately, she can count on Theodora's discretion.

Helena waits until Theodora's audience drifts away before walking over to greet her. The two women make an odd couple standing side by side: Theodora tall and stately, her profile resembling that of the Borzoi who accompanies her everywhere; Helena tiny and bird-like, with tufts of hair that stand upright like a rooster's coxcomb. Mutt and Jeff, Helena thinks, seeing their reflection in a windowpane.

With Helena, Theodora's tone is more pragmatic. The two women are long past the need to impress one another, content simply to catch up. Helena now hears from Theodora that the Ohstroms have offered the use of their house during their absence to Walter Scalin, a fellow American down on his luck. Both women have known Walter for years, and have watched his downward slide with a mixture of compassion and exasperation.

"To think it's come to this," Theodora says, voicing dismay for both of them. "Dependent on the charity of others for a place to sleep."

Helena has avoided Walter recently, but in the past, in better days when they'd travelled in the same circles, she'd found him to be a pleasant and courteous companion. Hard times, however, can change a man, and often not for the better. She'll soon have a chance to find out more from Nerina, who will be sharing the Ohstroms' place with Walter for part of each day.

The Ohstroms have hired a water taxi — a *motoscafo* — to take them back to the house. There's room for six people on the boat, and Helena, Christophe, Annette and Theodora are invited to join them. Before boarding, Helena wraps her scarf over her hat, tying the loose ends under her chin to keep the hat from blowing away during the boat ride.

"I know I look like the Wife of Bath, my dears," she says, seeing herself reflected in Alice's mocking smile, "but I couldn't care less."

The sight of the water taxi, floating a good three feet from the quay, is daunting. Because of the unusually high water level in the canal, it's impossible for the boat to come any closer, the driver explains. To do so would run the risk of scraping the side of the boat against the quay.

"Looks like we may have to swim for it," Bill says.

He may be joking, but Helena feels that any attempt on her part to board the boat can only result in humiliation. The sight of Theodora vaulting the distance as nimbly as the Borzoi beside her confirms Helena's fear that such a feat is beyond her.

"I think I prefer to walk," she says, turning away from the group.

Before she can take another step, Christophe lifts her into the air and passes her over the water into the outstretched arms of the driver. "*Ecco Signora*," the driver says, setting her down gently on a seat inside the covered part of the boat.

Her indignation is appeased somewhat when she sees Annette and Alice being hoisted into the boat in a similar fashion, like sacks of potatoes.

"*La bella Venezia*," Alice says, tugging at her skirt, which has risen immodestly high above her knees during the manoeuvre. "Don't you just love it?"

When the boat arrives at the back entrance of the Ohstroms' house, Helena lifts her arms for Christophe, as docile as a tired child.

The house, filled with warmth and soft lights, is a welcoming sight. A dozen or so guests are scattered across the long living room, which traverses the length of the house. The sound of the rain splashing on the panes of tall windows makes the room feel cosy, despite its marble floor and high, ornate ceiling.

After the ordeal of arrival and the hours of standing at the gallery, Helena heads for the nearest comfortable chair with a view of the room. While Theodora, made of sterner stuff, circulates among the guests, her Borzoi — Dante — stretches out at Helena's feet, resting his long snout on her shoes. Helena is indifferent to dogs as a rule, but she appreciates Dante's reserved temperament, and rewards him with a pat on the head.

A handsome young man in a white shirt and black trousers approaches with a tray of champagne flutes. Another similarly clad young man circulates with a tray of hors d'oeuvres. Where is Nerina, Helena wonders, shouldn't she be helping out?

Alice, who's come to sit down beside her for a moment, giggles when she hears Helena's question. "I know. I barely recognize her myself. But there she is," she says, pointing across the room.

Helena's eyes are not what they used to be, but she realizes it's not her vision that's to blame as she examines the young woman Alice has pointed out. Dressed in a shimmering green outfit, her long hair piled on top of her head, Nerina blends in easily with the elegant women in the room.

"I thought it would be fun to pass her off as one of our guests," Alice says, looking pleased. "You know, just in case somebody felt like being nosy. We don't want the police getting word of an illegal immigrant working in the house. I've given her a cover story should anyone ask any questions: she's here on a student visa, studying art history. She looks pretty convincing, don't you think?"

Helena agrees, unable to find any trace of the timid young woman sweeping hair cuttings at Lorenzo's. Nerina's transformation goes beyond the change in appearance. Playing the part assigned to her tonight — moving about the room, sipping champagne, chatting with the Ohstroms' guests — she appears totally at ease, as if parties of this sort were part of her normal routine. Looking at her, Helena wonders what other hidden talents Nerina is keeping in reserve.

"What do you think of the gorgeous help tonight?" Alice asks, accepting a fresh glass of champagne from one of the waiters. "Nerina found them. Wasn't that resourceful of her?"

Marco, Helena thinks immediately. Surely Nerina wouldn't bring him back to the house, not after what happened. But the radiant smile on Nerina's face when she comes over to greet her stops Helena from voicing her suspicions. She doesn't have the heart to spoil Nerina's Cinderella moment. And it's not likely she'll get a straight answer, in any case.

Nerina's smile vanishes when she notices Dante, stretched out at Helena's feet.

"Don't be afraid," Helena says, trying to calm her. She's witnessed Nerina's phobic reaction to dogs in the past. "He's big, but he's as gentle as a kitten."

While Helena caresses the dog's head to demonstrate his good nature, Christophe joins them. "You're the girl who was in such a hurry the other day," he says, recognizing Nerina from their brief encounter outside the Ohstroms' house.

"Sorry, my English very bad," Nerina says, edging away.

Is it the dog or sudden shyness? Helena wonders, watching her abrupt retreat. It's likely she feels the illusion Alice has created for her will be shattered the moment she speaks, like a silent movie star unable to make the switch to talkies.

Christophe seems to be baffled as well. "Is it me, or did I say something wrong? This is the second time I've scared her off. Who is she?"

Helena decides to go along with Alice's charade. "Nothing to do with you. Nerina has just arrived here on a student visa, and may be a little overwhelmed."

Why spoil the game when there's no harm in it? It's not as if Christophe and Nerina are likely to meet again. He and Annette are flying back to Montreal tomorrow. Just as well, Helena thinks. Matchmaking is not a sideline she cares to pursue.

VI

Homeless in Venice

Walter Scalin waits for the sun to reach the terrace of the Café Regio before heading out for his morning coffee. As soon as he chooses his seat, Giorgio, the waiter, brings him his usual espresso and lingers for a moment to exchange a few pleasantries. Walter welcomes the opportunity to display his proficiency in Italian, if only to distinguish himself from the tourists at the other tables.

To avoid random conversation, he stares straight ahead, watching the morning procession across the Campo San Polo: children on their way to school, women laden with provisions from the open market nearby and the stately *passeggiata* of the elderly, with no particular destination.

There is a brisk turnover in the café at this hour of the day, and it's not long before Walter spots an abandoned copy of the *International Herald Tribune* — an indulgence he can no longer afford. Tilting his chair slightly, he sweeps the newspaper into his lap. Has Giorgio witnessed his deft manoeuvre? What if he has? Giorgio, Walter reasons, is more likely to think prudence than poverty.

The sound of barking interrupts his reading. Looking up, he recognizes Dante, Theodora's Borzoi, straining to pursue a flock of pigeons, and, close behind, Theodora herself, struggling to control the dog. To spare them both the strain of an awkward meeting, Walter quickly hides behind his paper.

Walter has known Theodora since the time he first arrived in Venice, equipped with a small inheritance and vague ideas of becoming a writer. His literary ambitions were soon abandoned, but the lure of Venice proved more enduring.

Introduced to Theodora at a party at the Guggenheim, he had found her impressive and resourceful. Hearing of his plans to settle in the city, she took him to see a large comfortable flat belonging to a Venetian diplomat who worked abroad. Walter signed a ten-year lease; when it ran out he renewed it, although the rent had more than doubled, along with the cost of everything else in Venice.

Theodora once again came to his aid, suggesting that he put himself and his flat to work. Thanks to her recommendations, his underground *pensione* soon attracted a steady stream of art historians, museum curators, scholars — all devoted admirers of his adopted city and the kind of people he would have been pleased to meet in any case.

Not that Walter had much time to converse with his distinguished guests. The duties of running a B&B kept him far too busy shopping, cleaning and doing laundry. But in the winter months, when the visitors left and the fog rolling in from the sea shrouded the city, Walter's life was his own again.

He was soon, forced to scramble year round. As income from his inheritance dwindled — the result of sluggish markets and unwise investments — and the switch from the lira to the euro continued to drive up prices, Walter found it increasingly difficult to make ends meet. He tried to keep his predicament to himself this time, but it wasn't long before Theodora, like everyone else in their circle, was aware of his struggles to keep afloat.

"Start cashing in your social IOUs," she advised him the next time they met. "There are a lot of rich, lonely women in Venice, and you know most of them. Time to make yourself useful."

A word or two well placed by Theodora and it wasn't long before Walter's phone began to ring with offers of work: taking the dog to the vet, performing occasional secretarial work, hanging a painting, fixing a leaky tap. "Husband for hire" was how one of the women referred to him, recommending him to a friend.

The realization of how low he'd fallen came home to him one miserable, rainy day as he escorted one of the widows to the train station, her suitcase resting on his head to keep it from dragging in the flooded streets, her terrified cat perched on top, clawing at his face while he struggled to keep his balance. In the midst of this sorry spectacle he caught a glimpse of Theodora, sitting near the window of a café he passed. He had no way of knowing if she'd seen him, but from then on, he has made a point of avoiding her.

Not that it matters. Theodora appears to have given up on him as well since the loss of his apartment — the landlord had somehow gotten wind of the illicit business he was running on the premises — and the beginning of his dismal trek from one spare room to the next.

Fortunately, his wanderings are now temporarily halted, thanks to the Ohstroms — a welcome reprieve just in the nick of time, that, with any luck, might turn into weeks, even months. What made the offer of asylum particularly gratifying was that Bill Ohstrom couched it as a favour Walter would be doing for him.

"You're a hard man to get a hold of," Bill had said, running into Walter at a vaporetto stop. He and Alice had been trying to reach Walter, he explained, to ask him to look after their place while they attended to family matters in New York. There was a maid who came in daily, but there had been some trouble a couple of months earlier, and they would feel better knowing Walter was there at night.

"It may be time for you to start thinking about going home, as well," Ohstrom added before they parted. "It's not as if you have anything going for you here. And a fresh start might be just the thing to turn your life around before it's too late."

Walter, grateful for the reprieve he'd just been granted, accepted the unsolicited advice without protest and promised to think about it.

For the time being, he has nothing more urgent to think about than what to have for lunch. On the way home, he stops at the fish market near the Rialto. The colourful display of glistening creatures smelling of the sea quickens his appetite, and he hurries to make his selection before the stalls close.

When he enters the house, the noise of the vacuum cleaner and television blasting simultaneously signals Nerina's presence. Her comings and goings are erratic; he never knows when to expect her.

She turns off the machines as soon as she catches sight of him and greets him with a big smile. "I have present for you. Birthday present."

"How did you know?" Walter asks, surprised. It's been a long time since anyone remembered his birthday. Even he has forgotten that the day has any special significance.

"Simple. I check your passport," she says, pleased with her ingenuity.

Taking his hand, she leads him to the room where he sleeps. On the bed, he sees half a dozen new boxer shorts, carefully arranged in a semicircle. Nerina picks up a pair and, placing it against her waist, wiggles her hips in a playful way.

Walter is both touched and amused. He's pretty sure Nerina knows he's gay, but she can't stop herself from flirting, even with him.

"Where did you get these?" he asks warily, noticing the Derek Rose label on the shorts.

Nerina has told him of the bargains she finds at Miracoli flea market, but these shorts are brand new. It is one thing to wonder how Nerina comes by the finds she uses to perk up her modest wardrobe — silk scarves, bits of jewellery — another matter to partake of what could be ill-gotten goods. The years of running an illegal *pensione* have convinced him he has no stomach for breaking the law.

Nerina ignores his question and reaches for his old shorts, which she displays as evidence of the real crime. "Look, look" she says, pointing to frayed elastic waistbands and sticking a finger through the holes where the well-worn fabric has given way. "No good, garbage." With one swift movement, she sweeps his tired undergarments from his drawer to the floor.

"Thank you. A very thoughtful gift," Walter says, deciding to be gracious. Nerina meant well, and he doubts the crime, if crime there is, can be undone. "Why don't you stay for dinner and help me celebrate my birthday."

Nerina claps her hands with delight. "I come back later and bring wine."

She's gone before he can tell her there's no need to bring anything. Bill Ohstrom has invited him to make use of the wine cellar whenever he feels like it. Tonight seems like a fitting occasion to take him up on his offer.

VII

Life class

Nerina starts to run as soon as she hits the street. She is late, always late, always chasing the clock. No matter how fast she moves, she will probably not reach the Scuola Internazionale del Arte in time for the start of the drawing class.

She hears the students' voices and their laughter echoing down from the top floor when she arrives. It doesn't sound as if they care that she's late. The raucous noise continues after she slips into the room, making her think her arrival has gone unnoticed. But once she steps behind the screen to change into the long red kimono provided for her, the scraping of chairs and the rustle of drawing paper indicate the students are getting ready for her appearance.

While she changes, she hears the teacher, Signor Perrone, instructing the students. "You are here to participate in a centuries-old tradition that goes back to the very beginning of art. The nude figure can express every aspect of humanity, from the heroic to the pathetic. Remember, it is the cornerstone of all art." It pleases her to think she is a part of this noble tradition.

Nerina slips out of her robe and takes up her pose in the raised chair facing the class. There are tape marks on the floor and on the sides of the chair to remind her where to place her arms and feet. Watching her, Signor Perrone nods to indicate she's hit the marks exactly. Behind her, music erupts from the CD player. English is the language of the classroom, but the music is always Venetian. Today, Signor Perrone has chosen one of Vivaldi's Mandolin Concerti.

When she had been asked if she had any experience posing for a life drawing class, she'd lied and said yes. What could be so difficult about undressing and holding a pose? It was just like the game called statue that she played as a child, she told herself — only without clothes. And that part would be no worse than undressing in a doctor's office.

She was only partially right. Posing nude is no big deal, but keeping still for twenty minutes at a time turned out to be surprisingly difficult. She does not see herself as fidgety, but now, after only a few minutes, every muscle in her body demands release. To distract herself, she watches the students work.

They are all about the same age — not much younger than she is — and mostly American. Although she doesn't participate much in their conversations, she likes being around them, listening to their light-hearted chatter — mostly about themselves — and pretending she's one of them. At the very least, her English is improving.

The room is quiet now and Nerina's gaze strays upward,

lingering on the high ceiling, the carved mouldings along the walls and the soft light filtering in through tall, dusty windows. The thought that no one knows she's here pleases her. She's proud to have found this job on her own and kept it secret. Keeping different parts of her life separate, as if there were a danger of cross-contamination, comes naturally to her.

Her mother was the same way. A Croatian Roman Catholic married to a Greek Orthodox Serb, she'd secretly had her daughter baptised a second time in her own church. Neither of her parents ever went to church, and Nerina never understood why her baptism — in any church — mattered to them.

Living with her maternal grandmother after her parents died, Nerina learned at an early age to avoid any mention of her father and his family. "Murderers, brutes," was how her grandmother referred to her Serbian in-laws. "I warned your mother not to marry a Serb, but she laughed and said, 'No one cares about such differences anymore.' I always knew it would end badly."

The truth was different, however. Nerina's parents had died a year after the ethnic war ended, in a car accident while on their way to Belgrade to attend her Serbian grandfather's funeral. Her father died instantly, but her mother survived long enough to be taken to a hospital in Belgrade, where she died several hours later from internal bleeding.

Her grandmother persisted in believing it was those hours spent in a Belgrade hospital that had killed Nerina's mother, not the drunk driver who had veered into the path of her parents' car. "The Serbs knew she was not one of them. They just left her to bleed to death like a dog in that hospital."

Nerina starts to count numbers, a trick she learned as a child whenever she wanted to block out her grandmother's voice. Over the years, the numbers have become the wagons of a train rushing past her as she counts: one, swoosh, two, swoosh, three, swoosh...

At the point when she feels she can't hold still any longer, Signor Perrone says, "Time for your break, Nerina." Leaving the room for the washroom, Nerina avoids the students' work. Looking at their drawings of her nude body makes her more uncomfortable than posing in front of them.

When she returns to the classroom, she sees that during her absence the easels have been rearranged to form a circle, with the drawings facing inward. She knows what this means: the weekly group critique. Which also means she can leave earlier. A lucky break; now she can keep her promise to meet Marco and still make it back to the house in time for Walter's birthday dinner.

She hasn't seen Marco in weeks, not since the incident with the brooch. He'd dropped out of sight shortly afterwards. Someone told her he had signed on to work on a cruise ship sailing the Mediterranean. When he finally called to tell her the ship was on its way back to Venice and asked her to meet him at the pier where it would dock, she was not surprised. By now she was used to Marco's habit of disappearing and resurfacing when it suited him.

From the start, when they first met at the University of Rijeka, the greater part of Marco's life seemed to take place elsewhere, away from the university. A few months later, when Marco managed to have himself expelled for trashing the office of his economics professor — "a lying bastard," according to him — he disappeared entirely. Months passed with no sign from him, and she assumed she'd never see him again. Then, a phone call from Venice, asking her to join him. There wasn't much to keep her in Rijeka by then. Her grandmother had died and she had been thinking of leaving for some time. When she made it to Venice, he was waiting for her at the Santa Lucia train station.

"We're only stopping for one night," he'd told her during his phone call from the ship. "So it's tomorrow, or not for a long time. I'll explain when I see you."

The warning of a long absence is sufficiently atypical of Marco to rouse her curiosity. There is also the fact that she has missed him, even though, after the incident with the brooch, she swore never to see him again.

The vaporetto lets her off at the San Basilio stop on the Giudecca Canal. It's only a few steps across a wooden footbridge to the Cruise Terminal, where Marco's ship, *The Black Pearl*, is docked. She's arrived on time to see the last of the passengers disembark, followed by the crew.

Looking at Marco as he walks towards her, his face deeply suntanned, his dark hair — much longer now — curving sleekly away from his forehead, Nerina reminds herself to keep her distance. She knows how easy it is to be swept up in the wake of the turbulence he creates. Marco, seems to thrive in chaos, moving from one act of recklessness to the next without any apparent damage.

"*Ciao bella*," he says, embracing her. "Even more beautiful than I remember."

It feels good to hear her own language again, but she resists him. "I can only stay a few minutes," she warns him. "I'm already late as it is."

"What kind of greeting is that? Come on, let me buy you a coffee."

"So, what's your big news?" she asks, once they're seated in the coffee bar. "You said you had something important to tell me."

"I do," Marco replies, taking his time. "You're not the only one in a hurry. My visa for the US has come through. I fly to New York tomorrow."

"How did that happen?" Nerina asks, trying to hide her dismay. Five minutes earlier she was determined to keep her distance from Marco. Now, his big news has left her feeling pathetically abandoned.

He has a sister living in New Jersey, he explains. After months of waiting, her request to bring him over has been granted.

"Don't be sad, Nerina. We still have tonight," he says, whispering the words in her ear.

"I'm surprised, not sad. You never mentioned a sister before."

"I hardly know her. She left home when I was still a kid. I wasn't even sure she'd answer my letter, but she came through in the end."

How is it that everyone has a relative in America except her? She's sliding dangerously close to self-pity, she realizes, and stands up to leave before she makes a fool of herself.

"Wait," Marco says. He grabs her arm with one hand, using the other to retrieve a small bag from his jacket pocket. "I brought you a gift from Sarandë, in Albania. The ship stopped there so the tourists could visit the remains of an ancient Greek city nearby. I decided to check out the live town instead. That's where I found this." He hands her the parcel. "Bet no one's ever brought you a gift from Albania before."

Nerina opens the bag and sees a pretty aquamarine necklace. It doesn't look particularly Albanian, not that she could tell if it did.

"Here, let me see how it looks on you," Marco says, lifting her hair off her neck to fasten the clasp. "Perfect," he says, stepping back to admire the result. "The colour matches your eyes exactly."

"Thank you," Nerina says, kissing him lightly.

"When will I see you?" he asks, his arms tightening around her.

She feels like crying, but she tries to keep her voice light. "I promised to celebrate a friend's birthday tonight. I'm not sure when I can get away."

"I'll be waiting," Marco replies, not bothering to ask about the friend. "A guy I know from back home — he's the one who helped me get a job on the ship — has arranged it so that we can use one of the luxury cabins tonight. I've got the key right here," he adds, displaying the evidence.

"I'll try," she says, although she knows she'll do as he asks. Keeping her distance doesn't seem as important right now. The way things are going she may never see him again. Her attempts to obtain a visa to the US have never felt more hopeless.

Marco knows she's coming as well. "See you soon," he says, his broad smile conveying utter confidence.

VIII

Walter's decision

The light outside is fading when Nerina reappears, bringing wine and eager to help. While Walter sets out the ingredients for their simple meal — sautéed squid and tomatoes over polenta — she busies herself with the table. Her aesthetic talents extend beyond her appearance, Walter notes, as he watches her fold napkins into the shape of birds and build a centrepiece from the geraniums and ivy cuttings that she's pilfered from the planters in the courtyard.

Nerina's mood turns darker once they're seated across from each other. She seems preoccupied and distant, not at all like the girl who danced around mocking his shabby underwear only hours earlier.

"Everything all right?" he asks, noticing she's not eating.

"Not hungry," she says, thinking he's asking about the food.

After several minutes of silence, she looks up at him and asks, "Why they not want me?"

Walter has no need to ask who "they" are. The subject of Nerina's complicated dealings with immigration officials comes up frequently. Her explanations are hard to follow, and all he really knows is that she is living in the country illegally — a difficult point of departure — and that the Ohstroms are trying to help. According to Bill, they were hoping to obtain a domestic employee visa for Nerina so they could take her with them the next time they returned to New York.

"Didn't the Ohstroms promise to help you?"

"Promises mean nothing. They forget about me."

"What's brought this on?" he asks, bewildered. He's never heard her sound so despondent. "Have they given you a reason to doubt them?"

Nerina shrugs and says nothing, concentrating on the unfurled bird, now a tight ball of linen that she rolls back and forth with the palm of her hand.

"These things take time," Walter says, trying to be encouraging. "I'm sure they're doing all they can." He has no idea if what he's said is true, but her unhappiness makes him uneasy.

Nerina looks at him for a long moment. "You American," she says. "Why you no help?"

"I wish I could, but what can I do?"

It's true he's in no position to help anyone, yet his answer leaves him feeling uncomfortable. He wishes he could rise to the occasion in some way, at least give her some useful advice, but the reproachful look in her eyes only makes him want to escape.

Nerina saves him the trouble. Rising from the table, she tells him she has to go meet a friend.

He's used to her sudden departures, yet he can't help feeling tonight she's fleeing from him. He has disappointed her, and disappointed himself as well.

He decides to take a walk to clear his head. Leaving behind the campo, crowded with people gathering for the evening's outdoor screening, he makes his way along quiet narrow streets where at this hour he's unlikely to meet anyone else.

He soon finds himself in the Dorsoduro quarter, in front of the illuminated dome of the Salute church. He savours the cool breeze rising off the lagoon for a few minutes before heading back. His route home takes him past the Guggenheim. Tonight, its rooms and grounds are brightly lit and crowded with people — mostly Americans, from the sound of the conversation.

Walter pulls back into the shadows, not wishing to be seen by the latest arrivals — Theodora and Helena — as they pause to show their invitations to the guard at the gate. It's no surprise to find that he's been dropped from the museum's invitation list for a second year in a row. He believed himself inured to the numerous minor humiliations that have become routine since news of his homelessness spread through the foreign community. The sense of weariness that sweeps over him now suggests otherwise. Dragging his feet up and down the steps of the many bridges along his route, he feels like an old man. No wonder he chose not to remember his birthday.

The soundtrack of the Chinese movie playing in the campo follows him inside the house. It does not prevent him from falling into an instant and profound sleep. When he hears a phone ring some time later, it takes him a few seconds to realize the jarring sound comes from his bedside table, not the screen.

"Sorry to wake you," he hears Bill Ohstrom say, "I must have miscalculated the time difference."

Walter glances at the bedside clock. He has slept less than an hour and the alertness he simulates requires an effort. His mind clears quickly, when he hears Bill tell him that he and Alice are coming back sooner than planned.

"The flat at the back of our house has suddenly become available," Bill explains. "We've been dying to get our hands on it to have direct access to the canal. Rotten timing for you, I'm afraid."

Only two weeks before he has to start scrambling again. He feels like a wounded animal forced into the wild too soon. He'd been counting on a long reprieve to rebuild his strength.

Getting back to sleep is out of the question. He wanders into the kitchen, hoping there's enough wine left to do the trick. He drinks the little that remains and starts to clear the table. Nerina's whimsical flower arrangement, a little wilted now, catches his eye.

For a moment he's struck by the similarity of their plight — castaways clinging to a precarious perch — but dismisses the thought as shameful. How can he compare his mostly self-inflicted troubles with Nerina's, which, given what he knows of her history, probably go back as far as she can remember?

"Why you no help?" she had asked him earlier. He had pretended not to understand, though he knew exactly what she meant. He may not have the power and influence of the Ohstroms, but even in his depleted state he is not without resources. He has a passport, a country — a country people like

Nerina are desperate to reach — and the luxury of being free to come and go as he chooses. From Nerina's perspective, these are inestimable riches. No wonder she turned to him for help

As the sleepless hours of the night tick by, the idea of marrying Nerina and taking her to America becomes the only desirable course open to him. How much more gratifying to act as Nerina's benefactor than to eke out his days at the mercy of his former friends' generosity. He has so little to lose, and Nerina so much to gain. And who knows, if Bill Ohstrom is right there may even be a chance for him as well. Whatever happens, it can't be any worse than what awaits him if he remains in Venice.

PART TWO

Smith Falls, N.Y.

IX
Prison

The snow has been coming down for days. Nerina, struggling through deep drifts to reach the mailbox by the side of the road, wonders what she is doing in this godforsaken place. It's a question she's asked herself almost every day in the months since she and Walter arrived in Smith Falls, a tiny village in the Northern Adirondacks.

She'd had her doubts even back in Venice, the first time Walter spoke of returning to live in the house that once belonged to his grandparents. "I have a feeling the place will change my luck," he told her. "I think that's what my grandmother had in mind when she left it to me — a second chance."

She was too overwhelmed by the generosity of Walter's proposal to say anything at the time. Besides, he knew more about the place than she did. Listening to him talk about it, she could see that he was filled with excitement by its possibilities.

"With no rent to pay and the cost of living much lower than

in the city, I'll be able to take my time figuring things out," Walter went on to explain in his usual slow, methodical way. "I've been thinking of using part of the house — it's a big barn of a place — to set up an antique business. I'm pretty good at spotting hidden treasures in piles of junk, and the practical skills I picked up working for the widows will come in handy. The area attracts a lot of visitors from New York and elsewhere."

Her first impression of the Adirondacks in late summer was reassuring. The landscape surrounding Smith Falls was as picturesque as Walter had described, and the spacious-looking house with its screened porch promised a pleasant change from her cramped quarters in Venice.

"Welcome to America," Walter said, leading her into the house.

A few days later, during one of their drives through the countryside, they came upon a sight dramatically at odds with its bucolic setting: a walled, concrete fortress, ringed by barbed wire, with an imposing tower at the entrance.

"What was that?" Nerina asked, as they sped by in the second-hand van Walter had purchased soon after their arrival.

"Pretty impressive, isn't it? That's the Clinton Correctional Facility, a maximum-security prison, known around here as Dannemora — that's the name of the town we're passing through. The inmates refer to it as Little Siberia."

The aptness of the name became apparent once winter set in. As one snowy day followed the next, with only Walter for company and the occasional crunch of snow tires from the rare passing car to break the silence, the house, surrounded by a frozen wilderness, felt more isolated than any place she'd ever known.

Their weekly shopping outings to Saranac Lake or Lake Placid offered little relief. The empty, snow-covered streets, where every second store and restaurant was either out of business or closed until better times, only intensified her feeling of having landed in a forgotten corner of the world.

Walter, however, appeared to thrive in his new surroundings, spending long, happy hours working on the house, or tinkering in the garage with the finds he had carted off from neighbouring attics, barns and church bazaars. A sign went up advertising his new business venture. It had failed to attract any customers so far, but Walter believed it was only a matter of time until things turned around. Business was bound to improve in the summer, he told her.

Nerina was not convinced. Walter's boyhood memories of the Adirondacks, swarming with vacationers in all seasons, bore no resemblance to what she saw around her: a burnt-out hotel, an overgrown golf course, yards littered with broken-down cars and rusted farm machinery. She doubted that summer would change things. According to a story she read in the Saranac paper, prisons are the only thriving enterprise in the region — seventy at the latest count. The article also said that while the inmate population is growing steadily, the surrounding areas are losing people.

She didn't see the point of discussing the article with Walter. Why discourage him when he seemed so happy? In any case, she planned to be gone by the time summer arrived.

While Walter worked in the garage, Nerina set her mind to mastering English. There was no TV in the house, but the ample supply of books — sturdy volumes of Robert Louis Stevenson's works and other nineteenth-century classics, intermingled with mouldy paperbacks left behind by summer visitors — offered a wide choice of reading matter.

She started with *Kidnapped* — recommended by Walter — but soon turned to *Peyton Place*, whose troubled heroines she found more compelling than Stevenson's dour Highlanders. The next book she picked, *Vanity Fair*, was more difficult, but the adventures of Becky Sharp held her attention. Each time she came across an unfamiliar word or phrase, she copied it into a notebook along with its dictionary definition. At night, she had Walter quiz her on her new vocabulary.

The hard work was paying off. One night, awakened by the banging of a loose window frame — Walter's next project — she realized that the argument she'd been having in her dream had been in English. When she told Walter about it over breakfast, he said it was time for her to learn how to drive. "It's all part of becoming an American," he assured her.

She went along with the idea if only to break the monotony of her day, but she couldn't concentrate. What was the point? From what she'd seen during her drives with Walter, there was nowhere she wanted to go. Instead of listening to Walter's directions, her mind drifted to the letter she planned to write to Helena when she got home. Her correspondence with her friend in Venice was her only link to the outside world.

This morning, when she reaches the mailbox, there are two letters for her. One is from Helena, her faithful correspondent; the other, from Marco, is a surprise. Despite his promise to stay in touch, she hasn't heard from him since he left Venice to join his sister in New Jersey. In the past she had waited for him to contact her, but loneliness drove her to break the rule and write to him at his sister's address. But as time went on with no word from him, she gave up waiting for a response.

Thick flakes of snow lick her face as she tears open Marco's letter. The confident tone is instantly familiar. While she's been stuck in Smith Falls, Marco has been moving on with his life. He has a place of his own now, in Astoria, Queens, and a job as a courier.

"*I'm on the go all day long,*" he writes, "*meeting all kinds of people, and I've gotten to know the city better than most natives. It's only a beginning, of course, until something better comes along. There's lots of opportunity here if you know your way around, and you know me, I'm a quick learner. Come and see for yourself. You must be pretty sick of the old guy by now. Any time you're ready, I'll give you a personal tour of the sights.*"

She puts the letter back in the envelope and looks up to find a pair of deer staring at her. Silent sentinels, their eyes follow her as she trudges back to the house. These are not the first deer she's seen close to the house, but she's still startled by their boldness. Walter says their growing numbers have forced the creatures into the open to look for food.

A week ago, they found a fawn dead by the side of the house. The ground was too frozen for burial, so she and Walter lifted the animal by its hooves and carried it into the woods beyond the house.

"I'm thinking of getting a dog," Walter said, after they deposited the animal at the foot of a spruce tree. "To keep the deer away from the house."

"No!" Nerina shouted, before she could stop herself. "Promise, no dogs."

"What's the matter with you? Don't tell me you're afraid of them."

"I was bitten by a dog once," she said in an attempt to justify her panic. There was no way she was going to tell Walter the truth about the packs of wild dogs that roamed the streets of Sarajevo during her childhood. The animals' owners had either been killed, or, unable to feed themselves, had abandoned their pets. Sometimes, when there were no people about, the snipers on the roofs of the buildings would use the animals for target practice, just to keep their hand in. She couldn't see the snipers, but the dogs were everywhere, even in her nightmares.

"Nerina is more afraid of dogs than snipers," her parents told their friends, as if her childish incomprehension of the real danger gave them some comfort.

The deer follow her with their eyes as she walks to the house. Thinking of what she will write to Marco, she's sure of one thing at least: there will be no mention of prisons, deer and empty roads going nowhere. Marco is too smug as it is.

X

Cashier

To leave Smith Falls, she needs money. That means finding a job. Her English is nearly fluent now and Marco's example spurs her on. There's no demand for couriers in this sparsely populated region, but when she and Walter were grocery shopping at the Grand Union in Saranac yesterday she noticed a sign in the window, saying the store needed a cashier. She called as soon as she got home.

This morning Walter is driving her to meet with the store manager. "Hurry up," he says, heading out to warm up the van. "You don't want to be late for your interview." Nerina tells him she'll be right there, but can't resist checking herself out one last time before leaving the house.

"Do I look all right?" she asks, as they pull out of the driveway.

"You look fine," he says, staring straight ahead. "You know, people around here don't spend much time worrying about their appearance."

She's noticed. Even Walter walks around now in jeans, flannel shirts, quilted vests and heavy work boots. His new style suits him, but unlike Walter she has no desire to blend in, not even for a short time. Today, a jaunty mauve beret, with matching scarf and gloves — hand-me-downs from Alice Ohstrom — add a note of frivolity to the bulky clothes she's forced to wear to keep from freezing. Her hands inside the fine leather gloves are already turning numb, but she doesn't care. The mauve accessories are her way of fighting the drabness that surrounds her.

The manager at the Grand Union turns out to be a middle-aged woman with straggly hair tied back with an elastic band, whose nametag identifies her as Doris. Sitting down across from her, Nerina finds herself being examined with unmistakeable curiosity. Perhaps the mauve touches were a mistake after all.

"You don't come from around here, do you?" Doris asks, handing her an application to fill out.

When Nerina hands it back to her a few minutes later, Doris rewards her with a warm smile. "So, you're the girl Walter Scalin married. We heard he came back from Italy with a wife. Now there's a place I'd like to visit someday. Maybe when I retire. My grandmother was Italian, you know."

Nerina doesn't mind passing for Italian. Walter has warned her not to go into any detail about her background. "Most people here have never even heard of Bosnia," he'd explained. "And those who have can't tell the good guys apart from the bad guys."

Discovering Nerina's connection to Walter has made Doris much friendlier. "I live just a couple of miles down the road from your place. It's good to see the old house being lived in again after all these years. Most of the time, when the old people die, their children close up the house, except for a couple of weeks in the summer at best. You planning to live here year round?"

Nerina evades the question, but she can tell she's passed the test. Doris is almost apologetic when she tells Nerina she can only offer her the evening shift, from five to eleven. "Even with jobs as scarce as they are in these parts, it's still hard to find people willing to work at night. The hours suit me just fine, but the young ones like to keep their evenings free for themselves. You and Walter are still practically newlyweds! Won't he mind?"

No problem, Nerina rushes to assure Doris. She and Walter are together all day long. "At least this way, he'll manage to get some work done while I'm at the store."

"Yeah, I remember what that was like," Doris says, sounding wistful. "Now, it's gotten so I can hardly wait for Ron to go off with his buddies on their hunting and fishing trips. He's a guard up in Dannemora and by the time he gets home, he's wiped. But hey, don't listen to me. Enjoy it while it lasts."

Nerina can hardly wait to tell Walter the good news. He looks pleased until she mentions Doris's name. "I knew her as a kid," he explains. "Her Dad used to do repairs for my grandparents. Too bad you stumbled onto her. I was hoping we could stay under the radar a while longer. Just watch what you say to her."

Nerina wants to say she knows better than he does how to appear friendly without giving anything away. Instead, she pretends to lock her lips with an invisible key and throw it away.

"I suppose I'll have to drive you back and forth every day. Lucky for you, I'm such a nice guy." Walter still sounds grumpy, but she can tell he's teasing her now.

"I'll arrange for rides with Doris," Nerina says. "We can share gas and lots of girl talk." The idea, which just came to her, strikes her as highly plausible. Doris's daily route takes her past Walter's house and she seems eager for company.

"As long as it's just girl talk. Good thing you spent so much time on *Peyton Place*."

Nerina's first day at work gets off to a shaky start when Doris tries to show her how to work the electronic cash register and the credit and debit card machines. It seems to take Nerina forever to process each customer, and she frequently has to stop and ask for assistance. It doesn't help that the clerk assigned to supervise her, Charlene, seems contemptuous when she has to show Nerina for the third time how to open the locked cash drawer.

Not only are the machines baffling, she doesn't recognize most of the food items gliding past her on the checkout counter. The Grand Union is nothing like the outdoor markets and small stores in Venice where she used to shop for the Ohstroms. She spends her lunch hour checking out the aisles of the store, trying to familiarize herself with products unknown to her: pop tarts, tortillas, endless varieties of cereals and soft drinks, an entire wall of frozen foods.

Most of the employees are young like Charlene, barely out of their teens, and seem to have known each other forever. When she goes outside for a cigarette break she finds them laughing and chattering together, a tight little clique. She might as well be invisible as far as they're concerned.

"You don't want to get too chummy with these kids," Doris says, lighting up beside her. "I've known most of them since they were in diapers. They're okay on their own, but as a group they get up to some pretty dumb things — racing cars, drinking, getting high on whatever they can get their hands on. Not that there's much else for them to do. The ones with any gumption get out of here as soon as they can."

Nerina is grateful for Doris's chattiness when they're driving back in her Toyota. Doris is the first person she's met since her arrival in Smith Falls, and she's curious about her life. In the first half hour of their drive, Doris tells Nerina about her husband's diabetes, her son's bitter divorce, the grandchildren she never sees anymore. Most of all, Doris is worried about her daughter, Stacey.

"Stacey always wanted to be a teacher, you know," she explains. "But the only job she could find was teaching inmates at the correctional facility in Malone. Those guys are so mean, they're kept locked up twenty-three out of twenty-four hours a day. The only contact Stacey has with them is through an opening at the top of the cell door, and she has to stand on a stool to reach it. What kind of a job is that for a young woman who dreamt of working with little kids?"

A car pulls out of a side road ahead of them, causing Doris to blast her car horn.

"I get such a kick every time I see one of those bumper stickers," she says, pointing to the rear of the car. "'Keep honking while I reload.' Get it?"

Nerina doesn't get it, but then this day has shown her she has a lot to learn about local customs. "You mean reload, like a gun?"

"Yeah. It's the kind of macho stuff guys around here go in for. I can't resist calling their bluff."

Doris honks the horn again as they pass the car, chuckling with pleasure.

"What if someone came at you with a gun?" Nerina asks, unable to see the humour in the situation.

"Nah, it's just a way of letting off steam. Everybody knows me around here. They know I like to kid around. Don't worry, you'll soon catch on."

Nerina is not exactly sure what Doris means, but after her disastrous day at work any words of encouragement are welcome.

XI

Zipping along

Filled with fresh resolve the next morning, Nerina finds that the intricacies of the machines under her command and the codes of the items sliding past her on the checkout counter are not as difficult to master as they seemed at first. Even disdainful Charlene offers a grudging compliment in passing. "Well look at you, zipping right along. What are you trying to do, make the rest of us look bad?"

Her newly acquired skills do not help her make any headway with Charlene or the other workers. Their smiles and greetings are friendly enough, but for the most part they ignore her, excluding her from the banter that goes on during breaks and the long lulls between customers. She gets the message: she is a stranger, passing through, here today, gone tomorrow. Not worth the time or effort.

Doris, on the other hand, grows friendlier by the day, inviting Nerina to join her for a smoke in the shelter of her car whenever the temperature is particularly frigid, and chatting non-stop during their drives to and from work. After several days of this camaraderie, Nerina is able to report to Walter that Doris is devoid of any curiosity about them. Doris's steady stream of words is restricted to what's on her mind on any given day, a field of concerns that flits from her aging cat to her children's unsatisfactory lives to her husband's sciatic nerve, which has been acting up again. Throughout all this, little is expected of Nerina except her company.

Two months into the job, Doris stops by at Nerina's counter to ask if she has any special plans for the coming weekend. The store is nearly empty of customers and the bright fluorescent lights overhead, turning night into day, offer no protection from what Nerina suspects is coming: an invitation to Doris's home.

Doris's next question suggests Nerina has jumped to the wrong conclusion. "You think Walter can spare you on Saturday?" she asks, taking a gulp of her Diet Coke. "This stuff will probably kill me, but I need the caffeine to keep going."

Nerina now guesses that Doris is probably checking to see if she's available to replace one of the cashiers. This is a more welcome request; she is glad for any chance to earn extra money. "Walter is going to a couple of estate sales in Lake Placid, I think. So I'm totally free," she says.

As soon as Doris speaks, she realizes she has misunderstood once again.

"Great," Doris says, looking pleased. "Stacey and I are driving up to Montreal tomorrow. She's been down in the dumps lately and could use a change of air. You two are about the same age and you'd be good company for each other. While you're out having fun, I can do a little shopping and take care of some business."

Nerina remembers hearing Helena speak of Montreal — her favourite city in Canada. At this point, after months of isolation, any city would be tempting, but there's no way she can risk crossing the border. If only she'd waited a moment before rushing to declare her availability.

"I can't go," she says, deciding she has no choice but to tell Doris the truth. "I'm still waiting for my temporary green card. I would need a re-entry permit to be allowed back into the US."

"No problem," Doris says, dismissing Nerina's objections. "We'll cross at Cannon Corners — one booth, very little traffic, and I know all the guards. If we have to, we'll smuggle you back in the trunk," she adds, looking pleased with herself.

Nerina has read about the smuggling that goes on at these small border crossings — cigarettes, alcohol, even people if they're willing to pay the right price. For all she knows, Doris, or her husband, may be involved in these kinds of activities. It's possible that, like Helena, Doris also has sidelines she doesn't discuss with everybody.

Whatever the case may be, Doris's cheerful readiness to break the law makes Nerina uneasy. "I appreciate the offer," she says, trying to sound as if she does, "I just can't take the chance of something going wrong."

"Suit yourself. I was only trying to do you a favour."

On Monday, when Doris picks her up as usual, Nerina asks how the trip went.

"We ended up not going," Doris says, offering no explanation.

Doris's unusual curtness makes Nerina feel she's being blamed for the failure of the trip. She tells herself she's imagining things, but in the days that follow she detects a definite coolness on Doris's part, as if Nerina has somehow disappointed her.

A couple of weeks later, when Nerina has managed to convince herself that she is indeed imagining the coolness — accounts of Doris's domestic dramas have resumed again during their drives — Doris drops by the checkout counter and asks Nerina to come by her office after she finishes her shift.

"Much as I hate to do this, I'm afraid I have to let you go," she says as soon as Nerina is seated across from her. "You can see for yourself how slow things are around here, and I've been told to cut back on staff. Anyway, it's not as if you really needed the money the way some of these kids do. You've got Walter to look after you. I hear he's a regular knight in shining armour."

What brought this on? Nerina wonders. Has Doris somehow found out the real reason why Walter married her? Unlikely, she tells herself. Unless Doris has figured out that Walter is gay and put two and two together.

"You're right," Nerina says, doing her best to sound unconcerned. "Walter's been asking me to help him get his business off the ground. Now I'll have the time to do that."

"Good. I'm not sure how much call there is for antiques around here, but you'll make out all right. You're a fast learner, not like these dumb kids stuck here forever."

The last remark doesn't feel like a compliment, but she no

longer cares. She just wants to get away from Doris's innuendos. "Thanks. Thanks for everything," she says, keeping her voice casual. "I enjoyed our drives together."

"You know where to find me."

Luckily Walter picked today to come into town for the pieces of lumber he needs, and is waiting for her in the parking lot behind the store.

"You did well to last as long as you did," he says when he hears the news. "With so few jobs around for the locals, I'm surprised Doris hired you in the first place. To tell you the truth, I'm relieved you won't be spending time with her anymore. She's a bit of a troublemaker."

With Doris's mystifying comments still fresh in her mind, Nerina thinks Walter may be right to mistrust Doris. It doesn't alter the fact, that she must now get started on the next phase of life sooner than she planned. It's true that she hasn't saved as much money as she would have liked, but she hopes Helena, or maybe the Ohstroms — whom she's contacted as well — will come up with some useful suggestions. Helena has promised to try to help, but so far there's been no response from the Ohstroms. Maybe her letter to them was lost or mislaid. She'll write to them again, she decides.

"I almost forgot," Walter says, as they pull into the driveway. "There was a phone call for you earlier."

"Who was it?" Nerina asks. Not for the first time, she finds herself growing impatient with Walter's slow way of speaking.

"Some guy named Marco. He left his cell number. Said you can reach him any time."

While Walter stores the new lumber in the garage, Nerina dials Marco's number. She can hear music and a woman's voice in the background when he answers. She's not surprised. Marco is never without female company for long.

"When are you coming?" he asks, as soon as he hears her voice. "I haven't seen you since Venice. Much too long."

She's surprised to hear him speaking so freely with a woman beside him. "I don't know. Soon I hope." Maybe the woman is a roommate, not a girlfriend.

"You can always stay with us," he says, adding to her confusion. "I'll pick you up at the bus station. Come soon."

When she turns off the light in her room that night, she sees a pair of deer in back of the house, looking up at her window. Don't count on me, she warns them through the glass. As soon as I'm gone, Walter will bring in the dogs to chase you away from here.

PART THREE

Manhattan

XII
Leaving

It's June when Nerina leaves Smith Falls. Through the window of the Trailways bus she can see rivulets of melting snow running down the mountainside and patches of green sprouting from the earth. A time for new beginnings. Nerina's thoughts, however, are back at the bus stop where she left Walter only a little while ago.

Saying goodbye had been harder than she'd expected. Watching him as he stood beside her, dressed in his woodsman camouflage, she couldn't help feeling she was running out on him. At least while she was around he had someone to talk to, someone with whom he could let down his guard. Not that Walter had ever expressed any regret about her leaving. For all she knew he might even be glad to have her out of the way.

To fill the silence while they waited in Saranac for her bus to arrive, she started to tell him how grateful she was for everything he had done for her.

"No need to thank me," he interrupted her. "What I did for you, I did for myself as well. Who knows where I might have ended up if you hadn't come along? Let's just say we're even. Anyway, it's not as if we're parting forever. I'll come and see you once you've settled, and you know you can visit here any time you like. I'll be here."

The next time she looks out the window, the mountains have given way to clusters of houses, and the bus is now moving in a cortege of cars and trucks. The trees are in full leaf here and clumps of wildflowers line the embankments. They must be close to Albany, where she is supposed to change buses. In less than three hours, she will be in New York.

Inside her purse is the key to her future — a letter from Helena that arrived a few days ago. She's read it so often she knows it by heart, but she pulls it out again just to bolster her confidence:

Please forgive my long silence. I have not forgotten you, but I thought it best not to raise your hopes before I had something definite to report.

After much thought, I finally decided to contact my cousin Leo Samuels on your behalf. Leo owns a framing store, where he exhibits some of his clients' work from time to time. He is well known in New York art circles, and I hoped that even if he could not use you himself, he would know someone who could.

Leo is a second cousin to be exact, and we haven't been in touch for years. One of those petty family squabbles that just grew in importance over time. For your sake, dear girl, I swallowed my pride and wrote to him.

I began with a note, congratulating him on a recent profile of him that I'd read in an art magazine I came across. To demonstrate my good will, I inquired about his mother, Miriam, although it was she who had been the cause of my estrangement from the family.

Leo's reply was quick and exceedingly gracious. Making no reference to the past, he wrote that he was coming to Venice on business, and invited me to have dinner with him at the Danieli, where he was staying.

We spent a surprisingly pleasant evening, and by the end of it I felt sufficiently comfortable to raise the subject of your predicament. Leo didn't seem the least bit put out by my request and immediately entered your name and telephone number in his Blackberry. He said he would contact you directly as soon as something turned up. I expect that you will hear from him very soon.

Nerina had had her doubts when she first read the letter, and wished that Helena had given her a way to contact her cousin directly. A few days later, Leo Samuels called, just as Helena had predicted.

"I don't normally hire people sight unseen," he said, getting right to the point. "But Helena spoke very highly of you, and the truth is I find myself in a bit of a bind." He explained that his receptionist had left suddenly and that he needed to replace her as soon as possible. He offered to put her up in a small room in back of the shop until she found a place of her own. "It's really a storage space, but I've had people staying there on and off for weeks at a time."

"I'll be there Thursday, the day after tomorrow," she told him, trying to sound cool and efficient — like a receptionist.

It's nearly eight hours since Nerina left Saranac and the bus is now making its way slowly through midtown Manhattan, crowded with more people than she's ever seen in one place. Looking out the window, her excitement builds as she recognizes the bright lights of Times Square and the profile of the Empire State Building in the distance.

When she steps off the bus in the Port Authority Terminal, she is overwhelmed by the noise and the rush of people in all directions. She stands uncertain for a moment, trying to get her bearings. There's no sign of Marco, who promised to be waiting for her when she arrived.

She's just about to panic when she sees him moving deftly through the crowd with the grace of a dancer.

"*Ciao bella*," he says, embracing her. "Sorry I'm late. New York traffic, you'll soon see what I mean."

He looks thinner and sleeker with his short hair and tight-fitting clothes. She has never been so happy to see him.

"Wild, isn't it?" he says, picking up her bags and guiding her towards an exit. "You'll get used to it in no time."

Nerina is not so sure. She stays close to Marco, afraid of losing him, though he seems to know exactly where he's going. A couple of blocks from the bus terminal he stops next to a small grey Honda.

"A friend's car," he explains, as he loads her bags into the trunk. "I borrowed it just for your arrival."

The car barely inches forward after Marco starts the engine. Police barriers block the road ahead, forcing the cars to divert to side streets. Beyond the barriers, a large crowd has gathered.

People stand with heads tilted back, their cameras pointed upwards.

"What are they looking at?" she asks.

"They're photographing the news ticker on top of the Times building," he says, pointing to the office tower ahead of them.

Looking up she reads: "MICHAEL JACKSON DEAD AT 51."

"Is it true?" she asks, watching the words crawl past her.

"Nothing else on the news since early afternoon. I guess you didn't hear about it on the bus."

The news is shocking, but so is Michael Jackson's age. She thinks of him still as the boyish young man in the music videos she loved to watch as a kid — much to her grandmother's annoyance. Her grandmother's case against the singer — that news reports of Jackson sending medical supplies to Sarajevo were pure fabrication, that he had no voice, and that, furthermore, all his famous dance moves were stolen from the French mime Marcel Marceau — meant nothing to Nerina. She had never heard of Marcel Marceau, and she didn't care what her grandmother thought. Yet all these years later, she can't help feeling vindicated by this huge public outpouring of grief.

"Will you look at that traffic," Marco says, pointing to the cars ahead of them. "Total gridlock. Never mind. It gives me a chance to explain a few things to you before we get to the house. Here's the situation. The woman I'm living with, Sarah, is the jealous type. Suspicious of every woman I mention. The only way I could think of bringing you home was to tell her you're my sister."

Nerina feels she's back on familiar ground. Marco may have learned how to navigate the streets of New York, but he's as lost as ever when it comes to his entanglements with women. "You'd better fill me in. Do we have other brothers and sisters? And what about our parents, are they alive?"

"No, there's just the two of us. Anyway, Sarah will be asleep when we get there. She usually leaves early for work, but if you run into her in the morning just pretend you don't understand her questions."

"I get it. I'm the dumb one in the family. Anyway, I thought you didn't like possessive women," she adds, teasing him.

"It's a long story," he replies with a show of weariness, as he manoeuvres into the middle lane. "I'll tell you all about it some other time. For now, just remember you're my sister and we're very close."

The apartment is dark when they arrive. As they tiptoe across the living room with the exaggerated caution of night time prowlers, Nerina starts to giggle. "What's so funny?" Marco asks once they're in the small guest room.

"Nothing," she whispers back, and again bursts out laughing.

"You're crazy, you know that?" he says, looking at her with a fondness that could get them into trouble.

"It runs in the family," she says, and pushes him out of the room.

Nerina stretches out on the bed and turns on the TV, muting the sound. She hasn't been near a television set since Venice, and she is riveted by what she sees on the screen. Every station is switching back and forth between images of the dead singer in happier times and the crowds gathered in cities around the world to mourn him.

As she drifts into sleep, she imagines her grandmother, arms crossed over her chest in disapproval, watching alongside her.

You were wrong, Baba, wrong about everything.

XIII

A room of her own

When Nerina wanders out of the guest room the next morning, she is relieved to find herself alone in the apartment. Last night's giddiness has worn off and she is in no mood to play the part of Marco's little sister. There's half a pot of coffee on the counter and a note from Marco. "*Help yourself to anything you like. I've left a map and some subway tokens on the chair in the hallway. See you later.*"

Glancing at the clock radio, she sees it's nearly eleven. She's slept almost twelve hours. Her appointment with Leo Samuels is not until three in the afternoon. Plenty of time to pull herself together and figure out how to get to his place on 3rd Avenue. She has some idea of the layout of Manhattan from Googling the city's streets on the computer in the Saranac Library. Picking up Marco's map, she sees that he has highlighted the route to her workplace.

Marco's thoughtfulness does not alter the fact that he has put her in an awkward situation. Why didn't he warn her when she called to say she was coming? How typical of him to present her with a fait accompli, leaving her no choice but to go along with his plan.

The strong coffee lifts her spirits. There is another option, she realizes, and she dials Samuels' number.

He sounds harassed and a little wary when she identifies herself. "I wasn't expecting you until this afternoon. Is there a problem?"

No problem, she assures him, she'll definitely be there. She's only calling to find out if she can move into the spare room this evening, rather than on Monday as they had previously arranged. "The people I'm staying with don't really have the space," she explains.

"I had hoped to have the room cleaned before you moved in," he replies, after a moment's hesitation. "But if you don't mind the mess, it's yours."

It's only a little after noon, but Nerina doesn't feel like hanging around the apartment until her appointment with Samuels. There is always the chance that Marco may turn up and try to talk her out of leaving.

It feels good to be out in the fresh air, and she decides to walk down to Samuels' place. It doesn't look that far on the map and she's got the time. After a few blocks, the weight of the suitcase begins to hurt her arm and she heads for the subway entrance. In less than thirty minutes, she finds herself outside Samuels' building, two hours ahead of her appointment with him.

The street is crowded with people rushing past her, as she stands uncertain what to do next. She decides to walk to a coffee shop she sees at the end of the block, but finds her way barred suddenly by a woman wearing several layers of clothing and pushing a grocery cart filled with garbage bags. She expects to be asked for money, but it's a cigarette the woman wants.

As Nerina rummages in her purse, she becomes aware of a man who's just emerged from the building and is looking at her with interest. She has no idea why she is drawing all this attention, and thinks it's best to move on.

She doesn't get very far. The man who's been staring at her has taken the dishevelled woman's place. "Nerina?"

She nods hesitantly. She's never seen this man before and has no idea how he knows her name.

"I'm Leo Samuels, Helena's cousin," he says, extending his hand. "I thought I recognized you from the photograph she showed me of the two of you. The suitcase clinched it."

"I'm sorry I'm so early. I'll come back later."

"Don't worry about it. I was just on my way out to lunch, but it can wait. Come upstairs, we'll talk there."

Leo Samuels turns out to be more affable in person than on the phone. He's also younger than she expected. For some reason she had pictured him to be Helena's age, but he looks to be somewhere in his mid-forties. Ignoring her protests, he takes charge of her bag, carrying it up a long flight of stairs and into a small office.

"Your English is much better than I expected," he says,

after they've chatted for a few minutes. "Helena gave me the impression it was pretty rudimentary."

"I've been working hard for the past year to improve it. But I still make mistakes."

"I'm certain you'll be able to handle the phones easily. Let me show you around and tell you a little about what we do here."

Samuels leads her into a large room lined with shelves. "This is the workshop where we build our frames," he says. There are three long tables in the centre of the room covered with strips of wood and metal, bits of moulding and a variety of tools in different sizes: saw blades, clamps, nail guns and others she can't identify. "I have a couple of assistants who do most of the framing," Samuels explains. "You'll meet them later on. They were here until late last night and took the day off.

"Here is our exhibition space," he continues, showing her into a long, windowless room, empty except for rows of canvases leaning against the wall. "Leftovers from the last group show, waiting to be picked up," he explains. "Some artists find it convenient to use my premises as a storage space. I should start charging them, but then they'd probably just abandon their works."

Finally, he leads her to a room at the end of the corridor. "You'll be staying here," he says, opening the door. Inside there are more canvases piled against the walls, a long metal clothes rack bisecting the room, an enormous armoire on which someone has painted an undulating green snake winding its way from top to bottom, a couple of armchairs shedding their stuffing and a blue futon resting on a wooden platform supported by bricks.

"I warned you it was a mess," Samuels says. "So is the bathroom next door. The boys can give you a hand tomorrow with some of the heavier things you may want to move."

"I like the snake," Nerina says, craning her head to take it all in.

"The work of one of your predecessors. Probably ruined a good piece of furniture, unless, of course, she becomes famous."

Nerina checks out the futon, which looks relatively clean. First thing tomorrow morning she will take it to the laundromat across the street, just to be on the safe side.

"Sure you want to stay here tonight? It's really pretty grimy."

Nerina assures him she'll be fine. It's been so long since she's had a place all to herself — Walter was careful to respect her privacy but she was still always aware of his presence. She doesn't care what the room looks like; just to be alone feels like the rarest of luxuries.

"I suppose you've known worse," he says. No doubt Helena has built up the desperate refugee part of her CV to prime Samuels' compassion. Nerina is not about to confirm or deny his comment.

Leaving her suitcase behind, she follows him back to the office. The phone rings, and with a tilt of the chin Samuels indicates he wants her to answer.

"Samuels' Framers," she responds tentatively. He hasn't told her what to say when answering the phone.

"Who the hell are you?" a woman's voice demands.

"The new receptionist."

"Well, Miss New Receptionist, get Leo on the phone right now. Tell him it's Meredith Covington. One of his damn frames has just returned from an exhibition in pieces."

"I'll check if he's here, Miss Covington," Nerina replies, feeling more confident. Rudeness has that effect on her. Turning around to look at Samuels, she sees him shaking his head and criss-crossing his hands in front of him in an unmistakeable show of refusal.

"I'm afraid he's left for the day."

"Shit! Make sure he calls me first thing in the morning."

"You handled that like a pro," Samuels tells her, beaming with approval. "Helena said you were a quick learner."

"She's been very good to me. I owe her a great deal."

"I have to tell you I was really surprised to hear from her. Until then, she was just someone in my mother's stories. They had been very close as children. This was before my grandparents left Poland — just in the nick of time, I might say. After the war, my mother traced Helena to Rome and tried to bring her to the States. Helena wasn't interested and the correspondence lapsed after that, except for the Jewish New Year cards my mother persisted in sending to her. It was her way of reminding Helena of her origins, which apparently she kept to herself once she settled in Italy."

Nerina can't recall any conversation with Helena about religion. The only time she came close was when she pointed to San Michele cemetery with its two churches, as they sailed past it in a vaporetto, saying this was where she wanted to be buried. Knowing Helena, it was probably an aesthetic choice, not an expression of a change of faith.

"We didn't speak of such things," Nerina says, feeling the need to defend her friend. "But I never had the feeling she was hiding something or pretending to be someone she wasn't. Why would she? She is very much admired in Venice, you know."

Leo does not look convinced. "That may be. But I find it interesting that she chose to make a new life for herself in a place where no one knew her, and to adopt her husband's Italian name, even though the marriage didn't last very long."

Nerina can sympathize with Helena's desire to wipe the slate clean. She herself doesn't go out of her way to tell people she was born in Sarajevo. She doesn't even like to hear about pre-war Sarajevo, where Catholics, Jews, Muslims and Greek Orthodox supposedly lived amicably side by side. It didn't prevent them, after all, from killing one another once the fighting started. Just because you're born in some unlucky place doesn't mean you have to carry it with you for the rest of your life.

She can't explain any of this to Samuels, but there's no need. The conversation is over as far as he's concerned. "Here is a set of keys to the place," he says, handing her an envelope with her name on it. "Be sure to lock both the upper and lower locks when you go out. There's a small fridge in the workroom and a microwave for heating things up. I've got to go make a home visit to a client — if I don't make it back I'll see you in the morning."

Nerina panics at the thought of handling the shop on her own, but the hours pass quickly and uneventfully. A few phone calls, a couple of people dropping in looking for Leo, and Leo himself calling to pick up his messages. If this is a sample of what's to come, the job should be a breeze.

In one of the quieter moments, she finds a piece of stationery with Leo's letterhead in his desk and writes to Helena to tell her how well things are working out. "*I'll never forget what you did for me,*" she adds at the end. Writing Helena's address on the envelope, she pictures the narrow canal running alongside Helena's street and her dusty flat high above the water. Vivid though these images are in Nerina's mind, they seem to belong to another life. For the first time in a long while, she is where she wants to be.

Near the end of the afternoon, Nerina calls Marco to tell him about the change of plans. She owes him that much, at least.

"Where are you?" she asks, the noise behind him making it almost impossible to hear him.

"In a bar, having a drink with friends. Come and join us, we'll get something to eat after. My treat."

"What about Sarah?" She's in no mood to play the little sister.

"In a meeting. Won't be home till much later."

"I don't know." Sneaking around while the girlfriend works doesn't appeal to her either.

"Come on. You don't want to spend your first night in New York alone."

He's right. And she still has to explain about moving out. "Ok. Tell me where you are and how to get there. I'll leave right away."

XIV
Big city

Nerina is amazed at how easy it is to find her way around in the city. Navigating the numbered grid of Manhattan is child's play after the twisting streets and alleys of Venice. The tempo of the streets is different as well. Each time she pauses to gaze at a gleaming tower ahead of her, she finds herself pummelled by pedestrians impatient to get past her.

She has no trouble finding the bar, but hesitates at the entrance, confused by the darkness and noise that greet her. Marco has spotted her, however, and waves his arms to attract her attention.

"What happened to the others?" she asks, although she's not altogether surprised to find him alone. Marco has never liked mixing his friends.

"They had to leave. You know Americans, always on the go."

As he helps her off with her coat, she feels his fingers trace a path down her spine. This too is predictable. "Don't do that," she says, pushing his hand away. "I'm not in the mood for your games."

"What's wrong?" he asks, with a look of concern that might convince people who know him less well than Nerina. "Aren't you happy to see me? We hardly had time to say two words to each other last night."

"Whose fault is that?" Nerina blurts out, regretting the words immediately. She had wanted to see how long it would take Marco to get around to explaining the surprise he'd sprung on her last night.

"Help!" he gasps, wrapping his hands around his neck and pretending to strangle himself. "Another jealous woman. What did I do to deserve this?"

Nerina laughs. She's not really mad at Marco, just a little annoyed to find herself caught up in one of his twisted plots. She should have known better. Marco has never made a secret of his habit of using his friends in his schemes. It was her mistake to think she was exempt.

"What will you have?" Marco asks, as a waitress comes to take her order.

"I'm starving. Can we order some food first, and then decide on the drinks? I haven't eaten anything since breakfast."

"In that case, let's get out of here," he says, getting to his feet. "There's a Korean restaurant half a block north of here. The food is pretty good and it's much quieter."

The restaurant he's chosen is half empty and the panels of cloth enclosing their table create an illusion of total privacy. Nerina has never had Korean food and she lets Marco choose for her. By the time the first dish arrives — bits of squid amidst strange-looking vegetables — she is so hungry that she grabs a forkful and stuffs it into her mouth. The shock of the spices hitting her tongue makes her eyes water and burns her throat.

"Drink," Marco orders, pushing a mug of liquid towards her.

"What is it?" she asks, once she can speak again.

"Barley tea. It cools the system."

They wait for the next course. "About Sarah," Marco begins, but fails to complete the sentence.

Nerina watches him fiddle with his chopsticks, enjoying his discomfort for a moment. "You were saying, about Sarah ..."

"Right. It's complicated. She's a really great person, but she's not like us. I couldn't tell her the truth. As long as she thinks you're my sister, everything will be all right."

Nerina wonders which truth exactly he's alluding to, but decides not to pursue it. "What's she like?" she asks, trying to sound neutral.

"Nice looking and very smart. She's with a big firm of chartered accountants that specializes in forensic work. Investigating fraud cases, insider trading, that kind of thing. Works crazy hours. We really only see each other on weekends."

"That's convenient."

"It's not like that," he protests. "I'm really trying not to screw this up."

"How come?" She's never known Marco to be concerned about how his behaviour affected others, especially the women in his life.

"I like her. I like living with her. And she can do a lot to help me get started. I don't plan on being a messenger for very long."

She feels a surge of affection, hearing the note of defiance in Marco's voice. "Nothing wrong with that," she says, patting his hand. "People like us need all the help we can get."

Marco gives her a grateful smile. "I knew you'd understand. Who knows, maybe Sarah will have some ideas for you as well. I can't wait for you to meet her. I know you'll like each other."

It's time to put an end to Marco's fantasy. "I'm sure we will, but I'm not meeting her as your sister."

"What do you mean?" he asks, his voice rising with impatience. "I've already told her you were my sister."

"It's simple," Nerina calmly replies. "She didn't see me last night, right? The next time we meet, you can introduce me as a friend from your university days back home. Tell her you ran into me by accident."

"That's crazy. How can I do that when you're staying with us?"

She recognizes the peevish look that comes over him when one of his schemes goes awry. "That's just it — I'm not staying with you. Not any longer. I moved out this afternoon." She enjoys the effect of her surprise as she informs him of her arrangement with Samuels.

"That's great for you, but how am I to explain to Sarah the sudden disappearance of my sister?"

"I'm sure you'll think of something," she says, turning her attention to the platters of uncooked meat and vegetables being set before them. "Are we supposed to eat this stuff raw?"

"I'll be your chef tonight," Marco says, clicking his chopsticks together in the air like castanets. She's forgotten how quickly he gets over disappointments. In a few minutes, strips of beef and vegetables are sizzling on the surface of the charcoal grill set in the middle of the table.

"By the way, you'll never guess where I delivered a package last week," he says, placing the first cooked morsels on her plate. "To the Ohstroms, the people you worked for in Venice. I can tell you they live as well here as they do in Venice."

"You're sure no one recognized you?" The thought of Marco near the Ohstroms fills her with uneasiness, while also reminding her of their failure to answer her letters.

"They weren't home. A housekeeper signed for the package. Anyway, why would they recognize me? You made sure I only came to the house when they were away. Remember? I still think we should have kept that piece of jewellery, you know. Rich people are always well insured, and you and I could have used the money."

"I thought you're turning over a new leaf for Sarah," Nerina reminds him.

"I'm just saying, these people are filthy rich. You should see the art they have in that house. It's like a goddamn museum."

"Don't get any crazy ideas," she warns, noting his lingering resentment about the brooch she forced him to return. "You want to get us both deported?"

"Relax. If you're not going to be my sister any longer, you can't tell me what to do."

She knows he's kidding, but with Marco it's hard to tell.

She hopes his desire to hold on to Sarah will keep him in line.

After dinner, they walk down 3rd Avenue towards her new place. "Sarah sounds like a wonderful person," Nerina says, just to make sure his mind stays on safe ground. "You're lucky to have someone like her looking out for you."

"Yeah, she's great," he says, in an absentminded way.

What does seem to interest him at the moment becomes apparent when they reach the door of her building, and he makes a stab at getting himself invited upstairs.

"Come on Nerina, it's been a long time. And after all these months of being stuck in the sticks with a gay husband, don't you miss sex?"

"You're offering me a pity fuck, is that it?"

"Don't play tough with me. It doesn't suit you. You know I'm the best, not to mention the only, friend you have here."

He's right, but it doesn't soften her heart. "Go home," she says, pushing him away. "Sarah is probably waiting for you. You don't want to make her suspicious, do you?"

"Ok. If that's the way you want it. I'll see you around."

She forgets about Marco once she's upstairs. Looking around the crowded little room that is to be her new home, maybe for months to come, she tries to imagine her life unfolding here. The only familiar object is her suitcase, which once belonged to her mother. She remembers falling asleep with her head on its hard surface during the flight from Sarajevo in her parents' car.

As soon as she can spare the money, she will replace it with a new one.

XV

Meeting Edward

It's late summer, two and a half months since Nerina moved into the room at the back of Samuels' Framers. She hasn't done much to it since then, seeing the space as a temporary refuge not worth the bother of making more comfortable. It's not as if she spends much time in the room, except when she's asleep. And if Meredith Covington has her way, she'll be seeing even less of it.

Meredith is the woman whose irate phone call gave Nerina her first taste of what her job as Leo's receptionist might entail. Since then, Nerina has learned that Meredith is one of the few women painters whose large canvases fetch some of the highest prices in the current art market. She is also a daily presence in Leo's place — a convenient pit stop at the midpoint of her morning walks.

On the days when Leo is late in arriving, Nerina is obligated to step in, fetching Meredith her coffee and serving as an audience for her complaints. It doesn't matter that Nerina knows none of the people who are the source of Meredith's irritation on any given morning, or that Meredith's fragmented, staccato delivery makes it difficult for Nerina to understand her.

Meredith's rants seem not to require a response, giving Nerina ample opportunity to take in the odd assemblage of items that make up her walking outfit: black sneakers flecked with gold paint, tiger-striped leggings, a tight-fitting black tank top, an orange denim jacket tied above the waist and a Yankee baseball cap to top it all off. A tall, auburn-haired woman in her sixties, Meredith carries off the look with a regal confidence that reminds Nerina of Helena's friend Theodora. Like Theodora, Meredith is always accompanied by a large dog — an Afghan hound — named, according to Leo, after her ex-husband, Edward.

"She's had better luck exacting obedience from the dog than she did from his namesake," Leo said. He and Meredith have known each other for years, and, despite her volatile temper, have managed to remain on friendly terms during most of that time.

Meredith's tolerance of Nerina's presence does not extend to Jorge and Jean-Batiste, Leo's assistants, who earned her wrath when they failed to understand her instructions on where to hang a painting they were delivering from Leo's shop. The two men refer to her as "*la loca*" and make sure to stay out of her way. Twirling an index finger pointed at the forehead, they warn Nerina to be on her guard.

This morning, however, Meredith startled Nerina by offering

her a job in the evenings, after she's done at Leo's. The way Meredith described it, the work would consist of covering each canvas in a layer of colour to create a background for her to work on.

"No skill required," she told Nerina. "You just hold the brush and run it up and down. Really, a monkey could do it."

Nerina looked at Leo for guidance, but he kept his eyes fixed on his computer screen, leaving her on her own. "I'll have to think about it," she told Meredith, hoping Leo would be more forthcoming when they were alone.

"You have until five o'clock to make up your mind. Leo will give you the address, if you decide you're interested."

"I could use the extra money," Nerina says, when Meredith is gone. "And it's not as if I have anything better to do with my time. But I'm a little scared of her, and half the time I can't understand what she's saying."

"Who does?" Leo says. "It might be worth a try, though. She pays well, and you're bound to meet some interesting people. Meredith knows everyone in the art world, and she's pretty fascinating herself — if you can hang on long enough to find out. Meredith tends to go through assistants at a very rapid rate."

Steeled for the worst, Nerina presents herself at Meredith's place on 9th Street shortly before five. Meredith greets her with an air of indifference, as if there were never any doubt that Nerina would turn up. Nerina barely notices. She is too fascinated by what Meredith is wearing: a long black dress, draped over invisible coils that circle her body and undulate with every step she takes.

"I'm due at an opening at the Whitney tonight," she says, catching Nerina staring at her. "Come along. I'll show you where you'll be working."

As Nerina starts to follow Meredith's bobbing figure, the Afghan saunters in and lunges at her. "That's just Edward's way of saying hello," Meredith says, making no attempt to restrain the dog.

Nerina's tentative efforts to slide past the dog earn her a look of scorn from Meredith. The dog, meanwhile, getting into the spirit of the game, blocks her way in whichever direction she moves. She tries telling herself there were no Afghans in the roaming packs of dogs in Sarajevo, and Edward's long, shiny coat suggests pampering, not starvation, but none of it helps. She's back in the grip of her old childhood terror, unable to move.

"Oh, for God's sake," Meredith snaps in exasperation. She calls the dog to her side, rewarding its obedience with cooing words and kisses on the snout.

There is no trace of softness in her voice, when she turns back to Nerina. "This is Edward's home, and you'd better find some way of making friends with him. Otherwise, you won't be able to work here."

Just as Nerina is ready to bolt, the dog suddenly loses interest in her and saunters away without a backward glance.

With the path now clear, Nerina follows meekly as Meredith leads the way through the house. When they reach the living room, the sight of a bleeding Christ nailed to an immense cross that covers an entire wall stops Nerina in her tracks. After her humiliating scene with the dog, she doesn't dare ask questions.

"Spanish," Meredith says, following Nerina's gaze. "I found it by the side of the road near Córdoba, and had it shipped here."

When Nerina manages to tear herself away from the gory Christ, she finds her attention caught again by an equally striking object at the opposite end of the room: a long glass display case, shaped like a coffin. She glances warily inside, prepared for another macabre sight, and finds only a small package wrapped in brown paper, resting on a bed of dried rose petals. Nerina thinks it's probably an art piece, only it doesn't resemble any of Meredith's works.

"That's a parcel my son sent from India," Meredith says as they walk past the display. The brief explanation only heightens Nerina's curiosity. Perhaps Leo will be more forthcoming about the glass box and its contents.

The studio, a long, rectangular room lit by a skylight, is one flight up from the living space. Nerina finds its clutter of canvases, array of art supplies and paint-stained floor pleasantly reassuring after what she's seen of the rest of the house. Nothing ghoulish here to distract her from the work she's to do.

"Your job for tonight is to cover the canvas on the wall with a single layer of this greyish blue acrylic paint," Meredith says, pointing to one of the jars lined up on a worktable in the centre of the room. "Just one coat, and don't worry if it's uneven. I like irregularity in my backgrounds. Be sure and cover the entire canvas before you leave, so it can dry overnight. Shouldn't take you too long. And don't forget to take Edward for a walk. He'll let you know when he's ready."

Before Nerina can protest, Meredith hurries away, the hoops of her skirt trembling in unison.

She tries not to think about the dog while she does a few practise runs with the brush on a piece of cardboard. The bare canvas looms large and intimidating. Listening to music might help, she thinks, and she presses the play button on the CD player. The booming voice of an Italian tenor floods the room. She doesn't really like opera, but she doesn't feel she can afford the time to search for something more to her taste. Placing the stepladder in front of the canvas, she climbs to the top and starts to work.

She's just beginning to enjoy herself, when the slap of paws on the floor alerts her to Edward's return. Thankfully, the dog is no longer feeling playful, content to stretch out at the foot of the ladder looking as massive and inscrutable as a Sphinx. Maybe he's an opera fan, or maybe he's just grateful for the company. As the minutes pass with no startling moves on Edward's part, Nerina's anxiety diminishes.

When she's almost forgotten about the dog, he suddenly bolts up and begins to bark at her. Remembering Meredith's warning, Nerina guesses it's time for his walk.

"I hear you buddy," she tells him, trying to sound confident. "Just hold on a minute."

The dog seems to understand, and waits patiently as she comes down the ladder and dials Marco's number. She doesn't know what else to do. Marco understands her fear of dogs better than anyone.

"You're in luck," he says, after hearing a brief description of the problem. “I’m in your area and can be there in a few minutes.”

While they wait, Nerina continues to talk quietly to Edward in an attempt to keep both of them calm. It seems to work. If she didn’t know any better, she would say there is a glint of sympathy in the dog’s eyes as she describes the source of her panic: the fear-filled streets of her childhood, the recurrent nightmares of being chased by a pack of hungry, wild dogs. It feels good to be able to talk about it, even if it’s only to an animal. “You understand, Edward, I’ve got nothing against you personally. I’m just terrified of all dogs.”

The barking resumes when the doorbell rings and Marco enters, but he soon has the dog eating out of his hand. Literally.

“I always carry a couple of packages of Good Bites,” he says, pulling the snacks out of his pocket. “Grilled steak flavour. Dogs find it irresistible, which makes my job easier. Couriers are like postmen. We have to be prepared for anything.”

While Edward chews on his treats, Marco demonstrates how to attach the leash and how to use it to control the dog by tightening and loosening the collar. “You have to be firm. The important thing is to walk the dog, not to let the dog walk you.”

Once they’re outside, however, Nerina lets Edward take the lead. He knows the route better than she does, and it’s all she can do just to hold on to him. It seems to work. A moment later, he slows down to a more relaxed pace.

“You’ve been avoiding me,” Marco says, getting right to the point.

He's right. She has resisted calling him, although she's often been tempted — particularly on those nights when, wandering the crowded city streets by herself, she's felt like the loneliest person on the planet. But even then she's resisted, knowing that starting up again with Marco is not the solution. It would be like moving backwards in time. There's no way she can say that to him when he's just rushed to her rescue.

She talks instead about how busy she's been, describing long, hectic days with Leo and the rush to a second job in the evenings, hiding the fact that she's only just started working for Meredith.

Marco makes no effort to probe further. "I know," he says. "It's this crazy city. It keeps you running all the time."

"How's Sarah?" Nerina asks, eager to shift the conversation away from herself. "Things still going well between you?"

"I guess. She's pretty hard to read most of the time. Back home, you always knew when someone was mad at you. But Sarah holds things in. There's also the business about food."

"What do you mean?" Nerina asks, while Edward pauses to sniff the base of a tree lining the sidewalk.

"Sarah's a vegan," Marco replies, making a face. "You know what that is?"

"She doesn't eat meat?"

"No meat, no fish, no eggs, no cheese, not even wine, sugar or honey. Her diet reminds me of what people lived on during the siege of Sarajevo — beans, potatoes, cabbage and bread — if they were lucky."

"Does she expect you to eat like her?" Edward is on the move again, with Nerina and Marco trotting behind him to keep up.

Fortunately, a tantalizing new smell soon slows his pace, while he searches for its source.

"No, but I can tell it disgusts her when I don't. So I pretend to like the lentil stews she prepares, and make up for it when I'm away from the house. Only it's not so simple. Sarah says people who eat meat smell differently. This means using lots of deodorant and mouth wash. You'd think I was cheating on her, trying to remove the scent of another woman instead of the smell of a hamburger."

The look of indignation on Marco's face makes her laugh. "You can always sneak into the bathroom and chew on a Good Bite when you've had your fill of lentils. That grilled steak flavour sounds delicious."

Marco punches her playfully on the arm, causing Edward to bark in protest.

"Looks like you made a new friend, Nerina."

She's amazed how good it makes her feel to hear those words.

XVI

Reunion

Figures begin to emerge against the monochrome backgrounds that Nerina prepares according to Meredith's instructions. Even in sketchy outline, these are people in torment — bodies floating in space, their limbs splayed as if contorted by some invisible force. The dark mood of the paintings gives new meaning to the gory Christ and the glass box every time Nerina walks past them.

Leo has told her that the glass box is a shrine; the package inside it, resting on a bed of dried rose petals, is the last thing Meredith received from her son before his death in India from a drug overdose.

"Her work moved in an entirely new direction after that. All her grief for her son went into her canvases. A review of her work at the time referred to her as 'the Queen of Misery,' and the label stuck. Not that it's done her any harm."

"When did her son die?"

"Nearly twenty years ago, but there is no shortage of suffering in the world to fuel Meredith's imagination. By the way, has she asked you about your memories of the war?"

"Meredith barely talks to me, except to give me instructions. Most of the time she just leaves notes telling me what she wants me to do."

Meredith's habits change as the date of the show approaches. She's home most nights now, working from early morning until exhaustion forces her to quit. She's even given up her morning walks, and it's fallen to Nerina to ensure that Edward gets his daily exercise. Although Meredith is more distant than ever, the dog greets her appearance with joyful exuberance, trembling with excitement as he waits for her to attach the leash to his collar.

Nerina is amazed to find how much friendlier people are when she's accompanied by the dog. The sight of Edward loping along beside her in a cloud of golden fleece brings a smile to people's faces. A few pause to ask questions — what's his name, how old is he, can I pat him? New Yorkers seem to have a soft spot for dogs, unlike their counterparts in the European cities she's known.

The dog seems to be having a good influence on her as well, she notices. The dreams of running from a pack of wild dogs that keeps gaining on her are becoming less frequent. It's possible she's sleeping better due to the exhaustion from working two jobs, but she prefers to give Edward the credit.

"That dog's better than a shrink," Marco exclaims, when Nerina tries out her theory on him during one of their telephone conversations. Now that Nerina has acquired a cell phone, they talk frequently. "And much cheaper, too. Dogs in America are definitely smarter than the ones we have back home."

"Laugh if you want. All I know is that I'm no longer waking up in the middle of the night with my heart pounding."

As Meredith becomes increasingly absorbed in her work, rarely leaving her studio, it falls to Nerina to make sure there's food in the house and a steady supply of the Château Margaux Meredith requires to fortify herself while she paints. She is also subject to sudden cravings — small rewards to ease the strain she is under — sending Nerina and Edward off on hunts to satisfy her desire of the moment: crystallized ginger, mango ice cream, kimchee, soy nuts dipped in wasabi — anything at either extreme of the sweet-salty taste spectrum.

During these expeditions, Nerina can't help noticing how much cell phone consultation goes on in the stores she frequents. It's true that the choices are staggering, but it seems strange to her that so many shoppers — men more often than women — require lengthy soundings before making a choice between different brands of mustard or different types of cereal.

There are no such distractions back at the house. Nerina is kept busy sorting through the letters, e-mails and telephone messages that accumulate each day "like fleas on a dog," according to Meredith. Requests for permission to reproduce her work in books, in magazines, on websites, even on CD covers and wine labels are set aside for Meredith's consideration when she takes a break from her work.

Looking as wan and pained as the creatures on her canvases,

Meredith greets each new appeal with deep sighs of exhaustion, making Nerina feel she's adding to Meredith's burden. It doesn't help that Meredith snaps with irritation whenever Nerina stumbles over the pronunciation of an unfamiliar word or name.

"Don't let her get to you," Leo tells her. "If all the attention she complains about dried up tomorrow, she'd be far more miserable. Just think of your time with her as valuable experience. It will open doors when you're ready to move on."

Heeding Leo's advice, Nerina agrees to come in on weekends as well as after work. Apart from Nerina, the only people Meredith still sees are her masseur and her gallery dealer. Even Edward has taken the hint to stay out of Meredith's way, and sticks close to Nerina's side.

Working seven days a week, Nerina has no time to fuss with her appearance, and considers herself lucky just to find clean clothes to put on in the mornings. Occasionally, she tries to sneak in a few of her most pressing errands while taking care of those assigned to her by Meredith. The most urgent item on her list this morning is finding a pair of shoes. All the walking with Edward has been hard on her footwear, and even harder on her feet. She's not ready yet for the chunky running shoes she sees on the feet of many New York women scurrying about town, but a pair of sturdy looking sandals in the window of a shoe store on 6th Avenue seems like an acceptable alternative.

She's about to enter the store when she hears someone call her name. She turns around and sees a man waving at her as he cuts through traffic to reach her side of the road.

She recognizes him at once. It's Christophe, Helena's Canadian protégé.

He embraces her as if they're old friends. "What a wonderful surprise," he says, beaming with pleasure. "The last time I saw you was in Venice, at the reception the Ohstroms gave following my exhibition."

Nerina's mind flashes back to the night of her transformation from housemaid to Cinderella. It seems so long ago. She can't believe Christophe has recognized her after all that time. Dressed in jeans and a cotton blouse, her hair pulled back in a ponytail, she bears little resemblance to the girl in the shimmering dress at the party.

Christophe looks the same, however. He's even wearing the same leather jacket he wore in Venice. "I had no idea you were in New York," he says. "When did you get here?"

"The day Michael Jackson died. Before that I was upstate."

"Helena told me you'd married an American. Does he come from up there?"

"Something like that. It's a long story."

Edward jumps up at this point and starts to bark — a sure sign he's ready to get going.

"That's a great-looking dog," Christophe says, bending down to stroke Edward's chest. "What's his name?"

"Edward. He belongs to Meredith Covington, the artist. I work as her assistant."

Christophe looks impressed. "Wow, that must be interesting. Listen, do you have time for a coffee? It's not every day you run into someone you thought you'd never see again."

The shoes can wait, Nerina decides, and she leads the way to a nearby restaurant with a few outside tables.

"Looks like they know you here," Christophe remarks when the waiter arrives with a bowl of water for Edward.

"We've come here a couple of times," she says, bending down to remove the dog's leash. "Edward makes friends easily."

When she looks up, she finds Christophe watching her attentively. "What?" she snaps. The scrutiny makes her uncomfortable.

"I just can't get over how different you are. In Venice, you looked Italian. Now, you could easily pass for an American."

"It's a refugee thing. We're good at blending in. Like chameleons."

"I can see that. Tell me, do you live in this neighbourhood?"

It's a simple, innocent question, but Nerina has to force herself to reply. It's been a long time since a man has shown interest in her; Marco and Leo don't really count. "Do you know the framing store on 3rd Avenue, just a couple of blocks from here? I work as a receptionist there. The owner, Leo Samuels, lets me stay in a spare room at the back. It was supposed to be a temporary arrangement, but I haven't had time to look for another place."

"I've heard of Samuels," Christophe nods. "He has a great reputation among artists. How did you end up working for two such interesting people?"

She's beginning to get the hang of it — the back and forth that pushes the door a little more ajar with each exchange. "I owe it all to Helena. She got me the job at Leo's and he introduced me to Meredith. She used to drop in at his place all the time, but since she started preparing for her new show she doesn't go anywhere anymore."

"That's understandable," Christophe says, leaning forward in his chair as if the conversation had suddenly become more private. "There's a lot riding on the success of her show. Money, prestige, reputation. It comes with the territory. Not that I'm anywhere in her league. At the moment I'm just barely getting by, but give me time and who knows? I'm already starting to make inroads with a few galleries. My luck could turn around at any moment."

Nerina recognizes the mixture of cockiness and insecurity she hears in Christophe's voice. A lot of the artists who come into Leo's shop are like him — eyeing each other with wariness and waiting for their big break. According to Leo, the attrition rate is high: "Many are called, but few are chosen."

"Is that why you moved to New York?" she asks, watching him fold his napkin into accordion pleats. His hands are big, thick-fingered, but still graceful.

Christophe gives her a rueful smile. "In a way. I was accepted for a six-month residency program for artists run by the Canadian government. Helena recommended me. I guess we're both indebted to her. When it was over, a Canadian artist I met here, Sam Frith, helped me find a sublet. He also hooked me up with a couple of guys in Brooklyn who let me share their workspace. Sam knew everyone in the art scene. Unfortunately, he's gone now."

"What happened to him? Did he die?" she asks, seeing Christophe's mournful expression.

"Almost as bad. He was forced out of his building when it went condo. A woman banker bought his loft and Sam moved to a small town in upstate New York. The last time I visited him there he showed me a copy of *Architectural Digest* featuring the conversion of his old loft. Sam's studio has been turned into a giant walk-in closet; the clothes inside are spaced out like trees along a walkway, no two ever touching. We had a laugh about it at the time, but I haven't had the heart to go back."

"It can get pretty lonely up there," Nerina says, realizing she's just opened the door a little wider.

Christophe gives her a curious look. She can tell he's winding up to ask her something — something personal — and she has a sudden urge to set the record straight.

"Walter, the guy I married, is gay. He offered to marry me so that I could come to the States. I was in a difficult situation and he was kind enough to want to help me. And while we're clearing things up, the story about me being an exchange student? That was just my cover for the party. The truth is I was an illegal alien when we met, working as a maid for the Ohstroms."

He seems silenced by her confession, but she has no time to wait for him to sort out his feelings. "I have to go," she says, reattaching Edward's leash. "Meredith is waiting for her lunch and I'm late as it is."

"Wait. When can I see you again? Can we fix a time now?"

Nerina hesitates. She wants to see him as well, but how? She'll have to come up with a pretty convincing reason to persuade Meredith to do without her for a few hours.

"Let me see what I can work out."

Christophe hands her the napkin he's been playing with. When she unfolds it, she sees that he's written his number in one of the crevices between the pleats. She folds it back again so that the writing disappears and slips it into her purse.

XVII

Hybrids

Nerina finds it easier to speak to Leo about taking time off. Unlike Meredith, Leo is not in the midst of an all-consuming project and is bound to be more sympathetic.

He is. "I've been wondering how long you could keep up this pace," he says, when she asks if she can leave earlier than usual. "How about tomorrow afternoon? The boys and I will manage without you."

When Leo fails to turn up after lunch the next day, Nerina is surprised by the intensity of her disappointment. All this distress about a missed date with a man she barely knows — and a struggling artist at that. Working at Leo's place, she's had many occasions to corroborate Helena's view of artists: driven, narcissistic, always dissatisfied. Yet here she is, anxiously watching the clock and wondering how long Christophe will wait for her.

It's nearly four in the afternoon when Leo reappears. His

meeting went longer than expected, he starts to explain, but she's not listening.

"You look really nice," he calls after her as she runs out the door.

It's hard to stay mad at Leo, but Nerina hangs on to the feeling for as long as she can. The anger helps to distract her from the nervous excitement she feels as she rushes to Christophe's place.

His sublet turns out to be a small, stuffy semi-basement on 24th Street. She's about to explain that she can't stay very long, but Christophe seems to understand they don't have much time. Without knowing exactly how she got there, she finds herself flat on her back on an air mattress, with Christophe beside her, his hot breath fanning her ear as his lips trace a path along her neck.

The swiftness of his approach takes her by surprise, but not unpleasantly so. To have matters taken out of her hands is strangely restful.

"I knew you were sensuous the first time I saw you," he says when she finally pulls away from him. The heat in the room makes it feel as if their skin has been stuck together with glue. The broken air conditioner in the window prevents any passing breeze from cooling the air, and the plastic covering of the air mattress maintains their body heat as effectively as an incubator. "I don't know if you remember. You were in a great hurry that day, running across the campo, but I could tell."

His satisfaction at being proven right makes her laugh. "I don't know about sensuous. Deprived is closer to the truth.

I haven't been with anyone for a long time. Anyway, you only saw me for a few seconds that day."

"It's your mouth. I noticed it right off. You can tell an awful lot about a woman from the shape of her lips."

"What are you, some kind of lip fetishist?" she asks, laughing.

"Absolutely," he says, with a hint of pride. "It's the first thing I check out in a woman."

She purses her lips out to resemble a caricature of a fish's mouth. "How do you like this? Does it turn you on?"

His answer is to pull her on top of him and swallow her mouth in his. The burning sensation of his skin is overwhelming and she feels as if her body were melting, dissolving, right down to her bones. Tears well up in her eyes and run down her face, mingling with sweat. She hopes Christophe won't notice the difference.

It's dusk when they emerge, but the air is still stifling. Christophe suggests a diner at the corner of his street. "Best souvlaki in town, with a powerful air conditioner to boot."

The place is just what he promised. Even the plastic-seated booth feels cool as she slides into it. She eats quickly, messily, liquid and bits of lettuce squishing between her fingers. When she comes back from washing her hands, Christophe is starting on his second souvlaki. She watches him fold back just enough of the aluminium foil to reveal one bite-sized portion at a time. When he's finished, he wipes the paper clean with his napkin and begins to fold it into a square that resembles a star. She has no idea why he does this. She knows nothing about him.

"I've been folding paper since I was a kid," he says, looking up. "My own crazy version of origami, I guess."

"Thank you for sharing that," Nerina says, only half mockingly. "Now for something even more important: do you realize I don't even know your last name?"

"Yeah, I guess we skipped that part," he says, with a teasing grin. "It's Dubé. Jean-Christophe Dubé, that's my full name. When I was in art school, I became aware how many artists in the past were known only by a single name — Michelangelo, Titian, Tintoretto, Caravaggio. I decided to follow their example. 'Aim high' was my motto."

"Dubé sounds French," she says, wanting more.

Christophe obliges. "On my dad's side," he explains. "But I'm really a hybrid. My dad is French-Canadian, Québécois, and my mother's people were Scots who settled in Toronto. I was born in Montreal, but we moved around a lot because of my dad's work for the Department of Foreign Affairs."

"Hybrid. That's an interesting way of putting it. I guess it applies to me as well. I'm half Serbian, half Bosnian." She watches his face to see his reaction; he doesn't look surprised.

"I know; Helena told me. That must have been a lethal mixture during the war."

"I don't really remember much. I was a child at the time." This is her usual response when she's asked about the war. Christophe, does not accept it as easily as others have.

"All right. We don't have to talk about it now, if you don't want to. But I can be very persistent, I warn you. I want to know everything about you."

His curiosity is making her uncomfortable. Christophe is moving too fast for her. She doesn't know yet if she's ready to trust him. In an attempt to steer the conversation towards neutral ground, she asks him about Montreal. "Isn't that where you were living when we met in Venice?"

"I returned to Montreal to go to art school. I was curious about the place. My father's family had lived there for generations. I arrived just before the 1995 referendum on Quebec independence, and found myself thrust into a crash course on history and politics. It was very easy to get swept up in the excitement of the moment."

"We had a referendum in Bosnia in 1992 and it didn't end so well," she says, breaking her resolve to divert his attention from herself. There must be something contagious about Christophe's easy, open manner.

"I know," he replies. "That's what makes Quebec so unusual. The independence side lost by less than one percent, but the night the results were announced there was only sadness on the losing side, no violence. I think that's when I decided to stay. There aren't too many places in the world today where people resolve their differences in such a peaceable way."

"It sounds too good to be true," she says, unconvinced.

"We'll go there together one day, and then you'll see for yourself," he says, unfazed. "I would love to show you around my native city."

"I'd like that," Nerina says cautiously. She doesn't know if the offer is sincere or a casual remark inspired by the moment. Marco is right. North Americans are hard to read. Learning the language is easy; its subtleties of meaning, however, remain stubbornly foreign.

XVIII

Heart attack

It's past midnight when Nerina returns from Meredith's place. The phone starts to ring as soon as she steps through the door. She rushes to answer, hoping it's Christophe. He hasn't been out of her thoughts since she left him in front of the Greek diner hours ago. Even Meredith, who usually pays no attention to Nerina except to give her orders, zeroed in on Nerina's distracted state.

"You have the concentration of a mosquito tonight," she complained when Nerina failed to catch something she'd said. "I don't care what you do on your own time, but while you're here I expect your mind to be entirely at my disposal."

The call is from Leo, not Christophe. "You're back. Good. I've been trying to reach you." He sounds anxious and tired and there is a strange beeping noise in the background.

"What's wrong? Where are you?"

"I'm at Mount Sinai Hospital with my mother," he explains.

"She collapsed in the subway this afternoon and they brought her here. The doctors don't know what's wrong with her. I'm going to stick around until I can find out. I just wanted to warn you I won't be in tomorrow morning."

Nerina has met Leo's mother, Miriam, on a couple of occasions when she's come by the shop to take Leo to lunch. A small, energetic woman, she had been a kindergarten teacher for many years, and she still had the sweet but firm manner of someone who has worked with small children. Miriam's sweetness extended to Nerina as well; she would inquire about how she was getting on, telling her to look after herself.

Leo is an only child and very close to his mother. Nerina has never heard him sound so distressed. She can't help thinking that Leo's bad news came while she was enjoying herself with Christophe. There's no real connection, but Leo's troubles dampen her pleasure in a way that Meredith's scolding failed to do.

"Don't worry about things here. I can cancel Meredith if you need me. I really hope your mother will be all right."

"Thanks, but it doesn't look good."

Despite the late hour Nerina calls Christophe, feeling the need to hear his voice. She tells him about Leo and his mother — but all the time she's really trying to find her way back to his room, where, for a little while earlier in the day, she had felt invulnerable to the damages of life.

Unfortunately, time has not stood still for Christophe either. In the hours they've been apart, an idea for a new work has captivated his attention, and he's eager to tell her about it. The idea, as far as she can gather, has something to do with their conversation about cultural hybrids.

"I've been looking for a way to use perceptual discrepancies and the fallibilities of memory to examine the way we construct what is real to us. The concept of hybridization struck me as a useful paradigm for the exploration of consciousness and the self."

Nerina has heard Leo mock this kind of high-minded talk used by some of the younger artists — gobbledegook, he calls it — and it makes her feel better about not understanding it. To hear Christophe describe his work in such opaque terms discourages her. Yet another language she must learn, if they are going to spend much time together.

"Stop. This is way too profound for me. Especially at this late hour."

"Sorry. I do my best work at night," he says, unfazed by her sarcasm. "I'll explain it all to you when you're not so tired."

"Can't wait."

Christophe has become aware that she's not happy with the way their conversation is going. "Come on Nerina, don't be cranky. You know I'm crazy about you."

The words melt her resistance. Before the conversation ends, she promises Christophe she'll find a way to see him tomorrow. She has no idea how she will keep her promise, given Leo's emergency, but she'll think of something.

Next morning, just to be on the safe side, she leaves a message for Meredith warning her that she'll be late. Even though she knows Meredith rarely listens to her messages, Nerina feels she's covered her tracks.

When Leo finally appears, he immediately flops into the chair across from her. It's clear that he's spent the last twenty-four hours at the hospital, and she doesn't have the heart to run out on him.

"The boys have just made a pot of their strong coffee. Shall I get you some?"

"I've had too much coffee as it is in the last twenty-four hours. What I need is to go home and take a shower. I just stopped by to see how things were going in the shop."

"Nothing for you to worry about," she assures him. "We're managing fine. How is your mother doing?"

"She's pretty banged up from her fall," he says, pausing for a moment as if trying first to sort out the story in his own mind. "It was caused by a heart attack according to her doctors. They say she's going to need bypass surgery, but first she has to recover from the fall before they can operate. To make matters worse, she won't hear of the operation. She says she's lived long enough and prefers to let nature take its course."

"She's probably in shock," Nerina says, trying to comfort him. "I bet she'll change her mind, once she gets used to the idea."

"Who knows? She's always been a stubborn woman, now more so than ever. The strange thing is she wants me to call Helena and ask her to come."

Leo is looking at her with an air of expectation. Maybe he thinks that as Helena's friend she can offer some insight. But she doesn't have a clue. Helena, she recalls, has little patience for her own or other people's illnesses.

"That is strange," she agrees. "Did she by any chance say why?"

"Beats me," Leo says, shrugging his shoulders. "They've been estranged as far back as I can remember. Now, suddenly, it's Helena she wants. I suppose it's the kind of thing people do when they think they're dying. You know, make peace with the past."

"What are you going to do?"

"I promised her I would call Helena tomorrow, but I doubt she'll agree to come. She didn't strike me as being all that interested in our family when we met in Venice."

Leo is probably right. As far as Nerina can remember, she's never heard Helena mention family in New York or anywhere else.

"I've been thinking," Leo goes on, "it might help if you were to call Helena as well. She is very fond of you, you know. What do you think?"

"Of course. I would love to see Helena again, but I'm not sure it will do much good. I've heard her say many times that she finds travelling more of an ordeal than a pleasure these days."

"Try anyway," he says, rising from his chair. "We'll compare notes tomorrow."

As soon as Leo leaves, Nerina rushes to Meredith's place. One look at Meredith's face and she can tell her message has gone unheard.

"Where have you been?" she demands, spitting out the words as if they carried an unpleasant taste. "Because of you, I had a terrible day. People knocking at the door, the phone ringing incessantly, and Edward has been going crazy waiting for you. You're supposed to be here, looking after things. How selfish of you to think of no one but yourself."

Nerina wants to point out that she is only an hour late, and cannot possibly be held responsible for Meredith's entire day, but Meredith's fury is impervious to reason. A small child in the throes of an all-out temper tantrum is how she looks to Nerina. To stifle her urge to laugh she buries her face in Edward's silky coat, and the dog, overjoyed, responds with a dance of ecstasy, jumping and twirling between the two women.

"Sit, Edward, sit," Meredith commands, using her most imperious tone, but the dog is too far gone to obey.

The sheer exuberance of his performance seems to melt some of Meredith's fury. A wan smile crosses her face, encouraging Nerina to speak.

"Leo's mother had a heart attack last night," she says, hoping to remind Meredith there is drama in other people's lives as well. And Leo is one of her oldest friends, after all. "He spent last night and most of today at the hospital with her. It looks pretty serious."

Meredith responds to the news with more irritation. "No surprise there. The woman eats like a pig. The one time I made the mistake of accepting an invitation to a holiday dinner at her house, the amount of food on that table was indecent. Which reminds me, I'm starving," she concludes without missing a beat.

"Tell me what you'd like and I'll go get it," Nerina calmly replies, but she decides on the spot to drop in on Christophe, no matter where she is sent. Meredith's cruelty is making her feel more selfish by the minute.

"Make sure Edward does his business," Meredith calls after her when she leaves. Nerina waves one of the plastic bags she now carries in her purse for such purposes and hurries away. It feels so good to be away from Meredith, even picking up Edward's turds seems pleasant in comparison.

She arrives at Christophe's door fifteen minutes later, out of breath and with Edward in tow. "I've got half an hour," she tells him and heads for the bedroom, with Edward close at her heels.

"What about the dog?" he asks, looking uncertain. "Can you leave him in the other room?"

"He won't bother us," Nerina says, taking hold of his hand and pulling him along. "He'll just munch the biscuits I've brought. They're his favourite kind."

"I don't know. I've never done it before with a dog watching."

"Just think of it as one of those perceptual discrepancies you spoke of last night," she says, forcing him down on the bed beside her. "You know, the reality of what we're about to do, and what Edward will make of it. It could be a paradigm for exploring different perspectives."

Christophe, to his credit, doesn't seem to mind Nerina's teasing. Or maybe he is too absorbed in undressing her to notice.

XIX

Helena arrives

To Leo and Nerina's surprise, Helena, after taking a day to make up her mind, agrees to come to New York to visit her ailing cousin.

"Leo was so helpful when I contacted him about you, I didn't have the heart to refuse him," she tells Nerina. "I don't know why Miriam is asking for me, but I'm hoping the visit will make up for my numerous sins — starting with my lack of enthusiasm when she wanted to sponsor me as an immigrant to the US."

At this very moment, while they are driving to Kennedy Airport to meet her, Helena is speeding towards them in an Alitalia jumbo jet.

"Maybe she's in one of those planes overhead," Nerina says, watching the steady stream of jets zooming in for landings. The traffic on the ground, however, moves at a discouragingly slow pace.

"Don't worry, we have plenty of time," Leo reassures her. "Even if she gets in ahead of us, she still has to go through customs and baggage claim."

Leo is right. Helena's plane has landed by the time they're inside the airport, but it takes almost and hour for its passengers to emerge into the area where Nerina and Leo are waiting. When Helena appears, her small figure barely visible in the throng of travellers, she looks older and frailer than Nerina remembers. It's been nearly two years since they've seen each other, but Nerina prefers to ascribe the changes to the fatigue of the long flight.

She throws her arms around her friend, ignoring for the moment Helena's dislike of physical displays of affection. This time, Helena does not pull away, and hugs her back.

"Let me look at you," she says, stepping back to check Nerina out.

Nerina suddenly wishes she'd had time to change out of the jeans and hoodie she's been wearing since this morning and into something more to Helena's liking. As it is, she only managed to tidy her hair and put on some lipstick on the way to the airport.

It doesn't help matters that Helena, wearing layers of soft grey jersey over black trousers and her signature black jet beads, looks as elegant stepping off the plane as she does in Venice, despite the rigours of the long flight.

"Is this what young women in Manhattan are wearing these days?" Helena asks, taking in Nerina's outfit. "I must say it looks very comfortable." There's a hint of mockery in her tone, but it's softened by the look of affection in her eyes.

"You're sure you won't change your mind and come and stay with us?" Leo asks Helena, as he hauls her luggage and shepherds the women to his car. "With the children away at school, there's plenty of room in our apartment. No need for you to go to a hotel."

"You're very kind," Helena says, struggling with the seatbelt in the back. "But I make it a point never to stay with anyone — one of the many eccentricities of a woman who's lived alone for many years. Too late to change now, I'm afraid."

The next time Nerina turns around to check on Helena, she sees she is sound asleep. The murmur of gentle snoring soon fills the car, and Leo whispers to Nerina, "I see the family resemblance now. She's as stubborn as my mother. They'll get along fine, these two tough old birds. That is, if they don't kill each other first."

Helena doesn't wake up until they pull up in front of her hotel on 39th Street. "Are we here? What a wonderful ride. I always sleep so well in a moving car. A pity one must leave Venice to enjoy such pleasures."

Leo reminds Helena he will be back in a couple of hours to pick her up. Nerina is invited to join them for an early dinner before they visit Miriam in the hospital. She is reluctant, however, to abandon Meredith in her time of crisis, despite her foul moods.

As the date of the opening draws near, Nerina has found herself increasingly caught up in the feverish pace of production that Meredith has set for herself. Watching the colours and forms emerge more distinctly each day is like watching the birth of a new constellation, one whose significance she can barely grasp, but which holds the power to relegate Meredith's outbursts of bad temper to mere background noise.

"It's all right," Helena says, as Nerina starts to apologize for deserting her on her first night in New York. "My return ticket is open-ended. We'll have plenty of time to catch up tomorrow, over lunch." She looks at Leo over the rim of her glasses. "I expect you let her have time off to eat?" she asks.

"No, not as a matter of rule," he says, feigning severity. "In your case, I'll make an exception."

"That's very kind of you," Helena replies, playing along. "One never knows about the customs of a strange land."

There is no trace of Helena's good mood when the two women meet for lunch the following day. "I've made a terrible mistake in agreeing to a reunion with my cousin," she announces, as soon as they are seated in a restaurant near the hotel.

There is so much Nerina wants to tell Helena, starting with the fact that she has been seeing Christophe, but she realizes that Helena's need to unburden herself is more pressing.

"Why? What happened?" she asks, curtailing her impatience.

"Reunions after a long separation are a bad idea in general," Helena sighs. "For one thing, there's the wreckage of time, more easily discernible in others than in ourselves. What really shocked me, was that the woman in the hospital bed was a dead ringer for our grandmother. Suddenly, I was thrust back even further into the past than I was prepared for."

Nerina thinks of her own grandmother, a woman embittered by the war, who rarely had anything good to say about anyone.

The likelihood of her ending up like her *baba* feels impossible, but, apparently, there is no controlling the alchemy of time.

"Then, as I leaned over to kiss her," Helena continues, "my jet necklace brushed against her cheek. She opened her eyes and said, 'I see you've taken to wearing a rosary now. All that's missing is the cross.' Crazy."

"You know, Miriam really wanted you to come," Nerina says, encouraged by Helena's chuckle. "Leo said that she continually asked for you."

"Wait, it gets better," Helena goes on, ignoring Nerina's comment. "'So you've finally decided to come and visit us,' Miriam said, after asking me to crank up the bed to a sitting position. 'Had I known all it would take was a heart attack, I would have arranged to have one sooner.' I know it sounds as if I'm describing a vaudeville act, but I have to tell you that when Leo said he was going to give us some time together, I panicked at the thought of being alone with her."

"You were probably spooked by the resemblance," Nerina says, trying to soften Helena's indignation.

"Only in part," Helena says, her tone indicating she is not ready yet to forego the pleasure of what she deems to be justified resentment. "Miriam can be relentless, particularly now that she's ill. Like many sick people, she thinks her condition entitles her to special dispensation, giving her the right to say anything that comes into her head."

"Didn't you try and stop her?" Nerina asks, finding it hard to imagine Helena as a passive listener.

Helena assumes an expression of innocent helplessness.

"What could I do? Short of slapping a pillow over her face, there was no way to shut her up. And what came out was all the bitterness towards me she's stored up over the years, starting with my original sin: when I chose to live in Italy, 'among strangers,' rather than be close to 'the only family I have in the world.' Sixty years later, she has still not forgiven me. Somehow, it's all tied up in her mind with my refusing to be part of the fold. You probably didn't know I was Jewish. Sometimes I forget about it myself. I have to say, it's not as if it's been a source of great joy in my life. Miriam, however, feels it's her duty to show me what I'm missing."

"How do you like your hotel?" Nerina asks, grasping for a less charged subject while Helena pauses to catch her breath.

"Don't get me started on that," Helena snaps. "For some bizarre reason, the entire staff seems to have been imported from Poland. Everyone, from the chambermaids, to the bellboys, to the doormen. I might as well be back in Warsaw."

Nerina laughs. "That's what I love about New York. All those different languages coming at you from all sides. It's great."

"Speaking of languages," Helena says, finally turning her attention to her salad. "I'm amazed at the progress you've made since Venice. Very impressive. How did you do it?"

Nerina, happy with the direction the conversation has taken, launches into a description of the months of isolation in Smith Falls, and of how she put them to good use, reading books and memorizing unfamiliar words or phrases. "*Vanity Fair* was one of my favourites. I still remember one of the sentences I copied out of it: 'She had the dismal precocity of poverty.'"

"Yes, I can see how that would appeal to you," Helena says, looking at Nerina with affection. "Substitute the word 'war' for 'poverty' and you have the same result. I take objection to the word 'dismal,' however. Precocity, no matter how hard-earned, is always an advantage."

Nerina is tempted to say this is something she and Helena have in common — the bracing effect of early exposure to war — but she doubts Helena is in a mood to hear it. And there is so much more to tell.

When she comes to the part about working for Meredith, Helena grimaces. "Some people take her almost as seriously as she takes herself, but I'm not one of them. The Ohstroms, who've bought some of her work, say she's quite a character. Bill and Alice would certainly be interested to hear about your experience with her. I'm surprised you haven't been in touch with them."

"I wrote to them when I was living in Smith Falls, but they never answered."

"The rich can be fickle," Helena says, with a sigh of resignation. "Too many pleasant distractions at their disposal. I'm afraid it's a case of out of sight, out of mind. But in their own way, they're very fond of you."

"Never mind about the Ohstroms, Helena," Nerina interrupts. "I don't really care anymore. There's someone else we knew in Venice who's reappeared in my life. You remember Christophe? The Canadian artist? He's living in New York now."

Helena gives her a startled look. "Really? How did that come about?"

"Pure chance. We simply ran into one another on 6th Avenue one day. We've been seeing a lot of each other since then."

"It really is a small world, isn't it?" Helena says, looking a little shaken. "I must say, it never occurred to me you two might end up together. That's why I went along with Alice's game to pass you off as an exchange student. He knows the truth now, I presume?"

"I know," Nerina agrees, laughing. "I couldn't believe he recognized me after all this time. And yes, I've come clean about my entire shady past."

"Just exactly how friendly have you and Christophe become?" Helena asks, looking closely at Nerina's face.

Nerina feels herself blushing as she tries to think of a way to satisfy Helena's curiosity without giving too much away.

"I see, that friendly," Helena says, indicating Nerina has already revealed too much. "My poor girl, I've warned you numerous times: falling for an artist is a big mistake. You'll always come far behind his work. I speak from experience."

"I have another confession, Helena: he's not the only new love in my life," Nerina says, racing past Helena's warning to safer ground. "There's also Edward, Meredith's dog. The most beautiful creature you've ever seen."

"I thought you were afraid of dogs," Helena says, pushing aside her salad. "I'd forgotten about the size of American servings. We could have easily shared this between the two of us. Anyway, remember how terrified you were of Dante, Theodora's Borzoi?"

"I know, but thanks to Edward, the fear is gone. I think of him as my therapy dog."

"Well, you certainly sound much more lighthearted than I remember."

Nerina guesses the remark is not meant as a compliment. "You say that as if it's a bad thing."

"I'm not a fan of the American brand of mindless optimism. It's the refuge of fools."

"Thanks a lot," Nerina says, her laugh more self-conscious now. "May I remind you that when I went to work for the Ohstroms, you were the one who told me Americans like people who smile a lot? But I'll try to be grimmer the next time we meet."

"Don't pay any attention to me," Helena says, sounding contrite. "I'm just a cranky old woman. This business with Miriam has left me more out of sorts than usual."

XX

Surprises

Leo reports that relations between the two elderly cousins have taken a slight turn for the better. Miriam, having purged her heart of her long-held resentment towards Helena, appears to have run out of things to say. Helena, for her part, has chosen to interpret Miriam's silence as signalling a truce.

In the spirit of forgiveness, she has taken it upon herself to persuade Miriam to have the surgery her doctors consider essential to keeping her alive. She has her own reasons as well. It annoys Helena that Miriam, who's only a year older than her, is ready to give up on life.

"If you believe as strongly as you claim in the life you've chosen, then why are you so eager to depart from it?" she asks.

Good point, Leo thinks, overhearing the question when he arrives for a short visit. It goes unanswered, as his mother continues to lie with eyes half shut, ignoring Helena's challenge — and everything else.

Leo has spoken to the doctor about his mother's low spirits, and was told that depression is not unusual following a heart attack. It would likely resolve itself on its own, but it troubles Leo to see his lively mother so depleted. He visits daily, trying to rouse her.

This time, he has brought a shoebox filled with old photographs that he found on an upper shelf in her closet. A quick glance into the box's contents revealed several charming photographs of the cousins as young girls, wearing identical taffeta bows in their hair, their arms entwined around each other's waists. He doubts his mother has looked at them in years, and he's pretty certain Helena has never seen them.

"It seemed to do the trick, at least for a little while," he tells Nerina back at the shop. "When I left, my mother was sitting up and she and Helena were busy correcting one another about where and when each photograph was taken."

Helena offers a different take on the visit when she talks to Nerina. "I avoid the pitfalls of nostalgia, as a rule — all that longing for an idealized past that never really existed. But Miriam has been so low lately I'm prepared to go along with anything that stirs her interest, however briefly. I can't believe I'm saying this, but I almost preferred her anger to the stupor she's fallen into now."

Nerina can only follow the story of the cousins in small instalments. Running between her two jobs, running between Christophe and Helena, she barely has time to catch her breath. Next to Meredith, however, she feels she has no right to complain. At least she's able to get some fresh air walking

Edward or rushing from one destination to the next. Whereas Meredith, as far as she can tell, has given up on sleeping, eating and all other activities that might take her away from her work. She looks frail, exhausted, the living embodiment of the suffering figures in her paintings.

"At the rate she's going, I'm not sure she'll make it to her own opening," she tells Leo.

"Don't worry. She'll make it on nervous energy alone, if nothing else. Right now, Meredith is operating in a heightened state of existence — like those people you read about, capable of feats of superhuman strength, like lifting a thirty-five-hundred-pound car to rescue a child trapped beneath it. Trust me, if she does collapse, it will be well after the opening."

"I guess you're right. I've just never met anyone with her kind of drive. It's sort of inspiring."

"Now you can understand why I find working with artists invigorating, even though they're often a real pain in the ass."

Listening to Leo, Nerina keeps an eye on the door. She is waiting for Walter, who's in town for the morning on some sort of mysterious business. "If it works out, I'll tell you all about it," he'd said when he called yesterday to let her know he was coming. She'd asked him to drop by Leo's when he was done, unable to find any other way to see him on such short notice. The idea of her two benefactors meeting pleases her, although she is nervous about how they will get on.

When Walter appears shortly before noon, she's surprised to see him in a suit and tie. It reminds her of his elegant appearance in Venice — so at odds at the time with his dire circumstances. "He's caught the Italian vice of *la bella figura*," was how Helena described it. "Putting your best foot forward on the way to disaster."

Walter looks much happier and more relaxed now than he did back then. "I guess the meeting went well?" Nerina asks, unable to contain her curiosity about what lies behind the obvious effort he's made to look his best.

"Looks promising," he says before turning his attention to Leo, who's come out of the back room to greet him. Walter requests a tour of the place, leaving Nerina wondering if he's trying to evade her questions. Or maybe, as a tool guy, he really wants to see Leo's workshop.

"You didn't tell me that Walter is interested in art," Leo says, when he and Walter rejoin Nerina.

"Strictly as an amateur," Walter replies. "Living in a city like Venice, all that beauty rubs off on you."

"Leo seems very decent," he says afterwards, as Nerina walks him to his car. "I can see now why you like working for him."

"He is. If you give me enough notice next time you plan to be in town, I'll arrange for us to have lunch together."

"Yeah, I'm sorry about that. It was a last-minute thing."

It's not like Walter to be so tight-lipped, but she restrains herself from asking any more questions. Walter, seems aware of her frustration. "All shall be revealed in due course," he says, giving her a warm hug. "I promise. In the meantime, stay in touch."

When she gets back to the office, she finds an invitation to Meredith's opening on her desk. She already has hers, and now, thanks to Leo, there's one for Christophe as well. He has told her several times how much he wants to attend the event. Everyone of importance in the New York art world will be there.

But when she stops by his place later in the day to drop off the invitation, he barely glances at it before setting it aside.

"Hey, I went to a lot of trouble to get that invite for you," she says.

"I know, and I appreciate it, but something unexpected has come up. It doesn't look like I'll be able to make it after all."

Nerina stares at him dumbfounded. Has life really sped up to the point where nothing makes sense anymore? "What do you mean? Why can't you make it?"

"Take it easy, Nerina," he says, taking her hand and lowering her gently into his ancient wicker armchair. Sitting on the floor across from her, he looks earnest and excited at the same time. "I was just about to explain. A couple of hours ago, I had a call from the owner of one of the best galleries in Montreal, offering me an exhibition. Sam, the guy I told you about, brought him around a while back to look at my work. He just called to say a space has suddenly opened up in his exhibition schedule and he wants me to take it. I was hoping you'd come by tonight so we could celebrate."

Nerina doesn't feel the least bit like celebrating. Surprises fill her with trepidation — experience has taught her to value the routine, the predictable — and she doesn't trust herself to respond to Christophe's good news.

Christophe has enough enthusiasm for both of them. He's thought of little else since the phone call, and is eager to tell her how he sees events unfolding. There's even a place for her in his plans.

"The work is leaving tomorrow by truck. I'll fly out tomorrow night or the next morning. As soon as the installation of the show is underway — two weeks at the most — I'll be back to get you. I want you with me at the opening. I'm thinking of driving back to Montreal. We can stretch the trip out over a couple of days and have a bit of a holiday. If you like, we can stop in Smith Falls and see Walter. I'm curious to meet him."

She doesn't bother to tell him she's just seen Walter. Listening to Christophe rattle on, she thinks this is the trouble with surprises, even well-intentioned ones: they take too much for granted, assuming you'll happily go along with what someone else has planned for you, just because it seemed like a good idea at the time.

"Stop," Nerina says, feeling overwhelmed. "This is much too much to take in, especially at this hour. I'm still having trouble adjusting to the idea that you're leaving tomorrow, and you've already moved on to Smith Falls and visiting Walter."

"You're right, I got a little carried away just now," Christophe says, looking contrite. "Take all the time you need. Just remember, this will be our first trip together."

She doesn't want to leave him with the impression of her bad humour on their last night together. Not trusting words, she moves to the floor and tries to connect to him in the way that's never failed them, hoping some of his enthusiasm will rub off on her.

Christophe is not altogether fooled. "You ok?" he asks, looking at her quizzically. "I know you're happy for me, but you've been very quiet tonight."

"It's to ward off the evil eye," she tells him, grasping at straws. "In my family, it was considered bad luck to talk about something good happening before it actually happened."

"We say, don't count your chickens before they hatch. Same thing, I guess. Come on, I'll take you home. You look exhausted."

When they say goodbye, she tries to put into her embrace all the things she's left unsaid. That she is happy for him, that she wishes him well, that she misses him already.

Tired though she is, she has trouble falling asleep and is awake when the phone rings. It's Marco.

"I've been trying to reach you all evening. Don't you check your messages?"

"I've been busy. What's up?"

"I'll tell you when I see you. It's important."

"I have to walk Edward at noon tomorrow. Meet me outside my building, we'll talk on the way."

She finds him waiting for her as soon as she steps out of her building the next day. He greets her with his usual confident grin, but falls silent once they start to walk. Marco is rarely at a loss for words, so whatever is on his mind now can't be good.

They're almost halfway to Meredith's place when he finally turns towards her to speak. "I'm in trouble Nerina, real trouble."

Marco is often given to overstatement, but something tells her this is different. "What kind of trouble?" she asks, not sure she really wants to hear the answer.

"I was caught leaving Bloomingdale's with something I hadn't paid for. They called the police and I've been charged with theft. The trial is in a couple of months."

Early in their friendship, when they were still in Rijeka, Marco had given her a Hermès silk scarf for her birthday, which he confessed he'd stolen. Many of her fellow students indulged in petty crimes in those days — a carryover from the lawlessness they had experienced as children — and Marco's habitual shoplifting was not unusual. Most grew out of it eventually, but after the incident with the brooch she should have known Marco was still at it.

"For God's sake, Marco, this isn't Rijeka. Didn't you realize you'd get caught?"

"It gets worse," he says, suddenly eager to make a full confession. "This isn't my first offence. I've been warned that the criminal charges against me can be used as grounds for revoking my visa and kicking me out of the country."

"Are you serious? That's terrible." Despite her anger at his stupidity, she feels a flicker of sympathy for him.

"I've got a lawyer. He's a friend of Sarah's and he's supposed to be one of the best."

"You mean she's helping you? She must be a very forgiving woman."

"Actually, she's furious. But she has her reasons."

"Like what? I can't imagine why she would want to help you when you've been so incredibly stupid."

"She's pregnant," he says, looking sheepish. The admission seems to embarrass him more than the crimes he has just confessed.

"The poor woman. You've certainly managed to screw up her life as well as yours."

"You've got it all wrong," Marco protests. "Getting pregnant was all her idea. She never even told me she'd gone off the pill. She says she knew I wouldn't agree, so she went ahead and tricked me."

"You're a total asshole," Nerina says, quickening her pace.

"Wait," Marco says, grabbing her arm to slow her down. "Give me a break. I'm not stupid enough to say that to her, especially now. In fact, my lawyer thinks that Sarah's pregnancy may actually help my case."

"You're still a total asshole. But I hope for Sarah's sake, and the baby's, they let you stay."

"Don't be so hard on me, Nerina. I really need your help now."

"Why? What can I do?" she asks, ready to crush whatever scheme Marco has come up with this time.

"You can testify as a character witness on my behalf. No one else here has known me as long as you have."

"You mean you want me to perjure myself. And what about Sarah? How will you explain my sudden appearance to her?"

"Leave that to me. I'll take care of Sarah."

"I don't know. There's a good chance I may be in Canada when your trial comes up." As she says this, Nerina realizes that Marco has managed to do one good thing for her. The next time she hears from Christophe, she will tell him how much she's looking forward to going away with him.

"I'll wait for you," Marco says, as they reach the front of Meredith's building. "We'll walk the dog together."

"Why? You want a character reference from him as well? I'll check his schedule and get back to you."

"Very funny. Don't forget, Nerina, we go back a long way." His eyes, fixed on her face, are willing her to remember.

He doesn't need to remind her. She's furious with him, but she knows that in the end she will do what she can to help him.

XXI

Meredith's opening

Nerina has asked Helena to accompany her to Meredith's opening. Despite her reservations about Meredith's work, Helena readily agrees. A festive occasion such as this one is bound to be a welcome change from the tedium of visiting her ailing cousin. Miriam is home now and more talkative, but their arguments have simply shifted ground. The subject of their disagreement now is Miriam's refusal to have the bypass surgery.

"She says she's leaving it all in God's hands," Helena tells Nerina as their taxi heads up Madison Avenue towards the gallery. "When I tell her God helps those who help themselves, she just gives me one of her infuriating saintly smiles — her way of saying I couldn't possibly understand. The strange part is that she has some sort of hold over me. Definite proof I made the right decision to put an ocean between us. Luckily, Leo is nothing like his mother. I suppose working with artists has mitigated her influence on him."

It surprises Nerina to learn that the two women have been spending so much time together. It's not like Helena to persist in a situation she finds so frustrating, but she thinks she understands. It's probably like the weakness that binds her to Marco — an attachment she's reluctant to sever, despite her ambivalent feelings for him.

"Perhaps you should see less of her," Nerina suggests. "From what you say, it doesn't sound as if she enjoys these arguments any more than you do."

"On the contrary. Whenever I make a move to leave, she asks, 'Are you going already?' in that guilt-inducing way she has. But let's not talk about Miriam any longer." The taxi pulls up in front of the building housing the gallery. "I'm determined to put her out of my mind tonight."

When they enter, the rooms inside the gallery are crowded and buzzing with excitement. It's been several years since Meredith's last exhibition, and there is a sense of festive anticipation in the air, as if something momentous and pleasurable is about to happen. The nature of the canvases on the walls, filled with suffering and torment, seems, in some perverse way, to heighten the celebratory mood in the room. Glancing at the paintings as they make their way slowly through the crowd, Nerina finds that they look different to her, almost as if she were seeing them for the first time.

"Art never looks as good as it does at an opening," Helena explains when Nerina mentions her reaction. "It's the Duchamp principle: place a urinal in a gallery and it becomes an important work of art."

Nerina is tempted to say that she's just read a book on Duchamp, suggested to her by Leo. At Nerina's request, Leo has compiled a list of books for her to read, as a basic introduction to modern art. Helena, however, has been skittish whenever Nerina's tried to engage her in conversation on the subject, as if talking about books on art fell outside the bounds of their friendship. This is not the place to change her mind.

Helena has already moved on to the next room. When Nerina catches up with her, she finds her speaking to Bill and Alice Ohstrom. Nerina knew they would be here tonight, but she's still taken aback to find herself in the presence of her former employers. She can't help thinking of the letters she sent them from Smith Falls.

If Alice remembers, there is no sign of it in her greeting. "There you are," she says. "I was hoping to run into you, but you can never tell in this crush."

"Nice to see you again, Nerina," Bill says, giving her a hug. "It's been a long time."

"Yes, why have you been avoiding us?" Alice asks.

Nerina doesn't know what to say, but it doesn't matter. Taking hold of her arm, Alice pulls her away from Bill and Helena. "Come along, it's time you and I had a little chat.

"Tell me, what's it like working for the great woman?" she asks, as soon as they're alone.

Nerina breathes a sigh of relief. For a moment there, she was worried what other probing questions Alice might have for her. Alice, is not interested in her after all, only in gossip about Meredith. While Alice grabs a fresh glass of wine off the tray of a passing waiter, Nerina tries to come up with some harmless anecdote to satisfy Alice's curiosity. But the sight of Meredith just ahead of them, dramatically resuscitated and surrounded by a circle of admirers, renders her speechless.

This impression of vitality is enhanced by the dress Meredith is wearing: silver-coloured, with horizontal pleats that march up the sleeves and the lower half of the skirt like a staircase that vibrates each time she moves, it seems to have a life of its own. Now the quivering dress is heading straight in her direction.

"Let's have it," Alice says, taking a big gulp of wine. "You know what they say, no man is hero to his valet."

Meredith is now just behind Alice, but Nerina can't think of any way to warn her except by keeping silent.

"Come on Nerina, stop holding out on me," she says, her voice rising with impatience.

But when Meredith appears in front of her, her recovery is seamless and swift. Turning on a dime, Alice's face and voice reflect only delight.

"I had no idea you two knew each other," Meredith says, making it sound like an indictment.

Nerina suddenly remembers Leo's earlier warning: be careful not to give Meredith reason to think you're monopolizing her important guests by chatting too long with any one of them. The likelihood of finding herself in such circumstances seemed remote at the time, but it occurs to her now that major collectors like Alice and Bill Ohstrom are in that category.

"I used to work for the Ohstroms in Venice, as their maid," Nerina blurts out, hoping the explanation will defuse Meredith's suspicion. She doesn't really want to stick around to find out. In her haste to get away from the two women she stumbles over someone's feet, almost losing her balance, only to have a strong arm steady her.

"Leo," she says, relieved to find him just behind her. "Is it all right if I stay with you for a while? Or are you one of those people I'm supposed to keep away from tonight?"

"Definitely not," Leo says, taking her arm. "You can hang out with me as long as you like."

As they make their way through the rooms, he points out the people who count as far Meredith is concerned: well-known artists, collectors, critics and museum curators.

"You'll notice they have that unmistakeable air of hauteur about them that makes it easy to pick them out, even in this crowd. The other clue is that they're constantly being sought out by admirers."

For all of Leo's claims about his lack of importance, he too appears to have his share of admirers eager to greet and exchange a few words with him. Nerina quickly loses track of the people Leo introduces her to, who, for the most part, barely glance at her before turning their attention back to him. Following him around, she feels like a child at a party for grownups.

"I've forgiven you for stepping on my toes back there, but my feet haven't," he says, steering her towards some chairs at the rear of the gallery. They sit silently for a moment, contemplating the large canvas on the wall facing them — a moody painting in twilight colours of a nude figure suspended in space.

Nerina waits for Leo to say something about the painting.

She likes the way he talks about art, pointing out details she would never notice and showing her how to look at a painting. It reminds her of learning to read, when all the dark little symbols suddenly began to form words. But when Leo speaks, it's clear his thoughts are elsewhere.

"I want to talk to you about Helena," he says, still looking straight ahead. "I'm starting to think her visit here was not such a good idea after all."

"Not a good idea for whose sake? Your mother's, or Helena's?" Nerina asks, Helena's earlier complaints still fresh in her mind.

"Probably for both of them," he replies. "Don't get me wrong. I admire Helena and enjoy her company, but I'm worried about the effect she's having on my mother. You see, these two women have been locked in a battle of wills for years, and now my mother's surgery has become the focus of their struggle."

"What's wrong with that? Maybe Helena can help change her mind about it. She can be very persuasive, you know."

Before Leo can respond, a man and woman wander in. They pause for a long moment, solemnly contemplating Meredith's painting.

"I wish it were that simple," he resumes once they leave. "But I fear Helena's arguments are having the opposite effect. My mother's resistance has grown stronger since Helena has taken to pressing her to have the operation. It's as if she's convinced herself that in heeding Helena's advice on this matter she's conceding that Helena may be right about other things as well — the way she's chosen to live her life, for example. It sounds crazy, I know, but I fear I'm right."

Seeing how grave Leo looks, Nerina treads cautiously. "Are you sure? Wasn't she refusing to have the surgery well before Helena arrived?"

"Look, she's been a healthy, energetic woman all her life. It was hard for her to accept the news that she was seriously ill. But I believe she would have come around after the initial shock wore off. I don't mean to be melodramatic, but I believe my mother's life is at stake here."

The degree of anxiety she hears in Leo's voice makes it hard not to take his concern seriously. "Alright. Do you want me to ask Helena to stop talking about the surgery? I think she would actually find it a relief."

"I'm not so sure. I think what we have here is a *folie à deux,* an insane desire on the part of each woman to prove the other one wrong — regardless of the cost."

"You mean to say your mother is willing to put her life in danger just to spite Helena?" Even as she poses the question, Nerina realizes how naïve it sounds.

"It's more than spite," Leo explains. "Helena's long estrangement from our family makes it difficult for my mother to trust her newfound concern. As for Helena, I believe she enjoys the opportunity to demonstrate that she is the more rational and reasonable one of the two."

This doesn't sound like her friend, but Nerina knows that the peculiarities of family relations can never be understood by outsiders.

"What do you intend to do about it?" she asks.

"I'm not sure. At the very least, I need to find out how long

Helena is planning to stay. I'm hoping you could help me with that. It might offend her if I just came right out and asked her myself."

"Of course," she readily agrees. "I'll do it tonight."

"I'm sorry to involve you in our messy family affairs," he says, as they rise to their feet.

"Don't worry about it. I'm glad to help."

An idea is forming at the back of Nerina's mind. If it works out, it may ease Leo's concern about Helena and his mother. For the moment, she prefers to keep it to herself.

XXII

Heading north

Nerina's plan falls into place more easily than she expected. When she tells Christophe about her idea of inviting Helena to accompany them to Montreal, he quickly agrees. Too quickly, Nerina feels, remembering how excited he was about the two of them going away together.

"It would be great to have Helena at my opening," he says. "She's a legend in Canadian art circles."

Nerina understands. She doesn't blame him for trying to take advantage of any help that comes his way. Working for Leo, she has learned that the odds of becoming a successful artist are no better than those of winning the national lottery. Making things nobody needs, wants or comprehends, trying to convince yourself that what you're doing is important and worth the sacrifices it entails, playing at make-believe when other people your age are living the life of adults — these are choices that call for desperate measures.

As for Leo, his face lights up as soon as he hears that Nerina's plan will give the cousins a break from each other. "This is a godsend, Nerina. Stay away for as long as you like."

Meredith has no objections as well when Nerina asks for time off. "I'm going away myself to visit friends in California," she says, sounding unusually serene. The positive response her exhibition has received — all the works in the show sold in the first days after the opening — appears to have improved her temper. The only gripe she has left is about Edward. "I was counting on you to take care of Edward while I'm away. Now I suppose I'll have to look for a reliable dog sitter. Poor Edward, he's grown so attached to you."

The guilt inducement works, with the added effect of making Nerina jealous as she pictures Edward with her replacement. For a crazy moment she considers taking the dog along on the trip, but she doubts Christophe would agree to it. Unlike Helena, Edward is no legend in any circle.

Only Helena herself proves difficult to convince. "I'd love to drive up to Montreal with you and Christophe, but there's Miriam to consider. I feel obligated to her, and to Leo. He did pay for my plane ticket after all."

"Leo knows about the trip," Nerina says, treading carefully. "He seems to think it's a good idea for you to join us. I got the impression he felt you and Miriam could use a respite from each other."

"Did he actually say that?" Helena sounds miffed. "I bet that's Miriam's doing. She shows no appreciation for all the trouble I've taken to talk some sense into her. I'm afraid if I run out on her now — because that's the way she'll see my departure — she'll just have another thing to hold against me."

"Why don't you talk it over with Leo?" Nerina suggests. "He'll know what's best for everyone involved."

Helena's scruples appear to have vanished the next time she and Nerina speak. "The dear boy is worried about me," she says, reporting on her conversation with Leo. "He knows how exhausting Miriam can be, and he will tell her the trip was his idea. After all, who knows when I'll have a chance to go to Montreal again? At my age, each voyage may be the last."

With Helena on board, there is still one more thing Nerina must do before she can leave: see Marco's lawyer. Riding the subway to her office on the Upper West Side, Nerina tries to think of all the good things she can say about Marco without running the danger of seriously perjuring herself.

The lawyer, a grey-haired woman with a friendly demeanour, has saved her the trouble. As Nerina reads through the affidavit prepared for her signature, she is relieved to find it contains little more than an account of her friendship with Marco, stressing the fact that he has been a caring and loyal friend to her. She can live with that, as well as with the last paragraph, which has her asserting that Marco has the potential to become a good father and deserves a second chance, if only for the sake of his unborn child.

Why not, she thinks as she signs the document. Deception is the rule in most immigration hearings, and people with worse crimes than pilfering in their résumé find their way into the country every day.

Christophe arrives home on the eve of their departure looking tired and preoccupied. "There is so much left to do," he tells Nerina, who is spending the night at his place so they can get an early start. "Mostly my fault, I guess. Seeing the work after months in storage has given me ideas for some last minute changes that I just can't ignore. So, naturally things are going slower than I anticipated."

Listening to him, Nerina feels that Christophe has changed as well. In the couple of weeks since she last saw him he seems to have become more focused, more serious, as if their previous months together had been a holiday interlude and now his real life has resumed.

She likes the change, she thinks. For one thing, it makes her want to be more serious about her own future. Since the marathon leading up to Meredith's show ended, she's had time to wonder about her next move. Much as she loves Edward, taking him for walks, running errands for Meredith and answering the phones at Leo's place no longer feels like a satisfying career path.

Helena is waiting in the lobby of her hotel when they arrive to pick her up. As she climbs into the back seat of Christophe's Honda on a rainy morning in October, Miriam seems far from her thoughts.

"I can't tell you how much I'm looking forward to this trip," she says, leaning back against the foam pillow she's brought for the long ride. "I don't mean to disparage the pleasures of your company, but what I'm really looking forward to is a good long nap as soon as the car starts moving." A few minutes after they've crossed the George Washington Bridge, Helena, true to her word, is fast asleep.

Despite her enthusiasm for cars, Helena made it clear before their departure that she would like to reach Montreal as soon as possible. There are people she's arranged to see, and, more importantly, her back will not withstand the rigours of an extended journey in the confines of a small car.

Christophe deferred to Helena's wishes, and the leisurely, meandering trip that he had first proposed, along with the cosy overnight stops, has been abandoned. The visit with Walter is all that remains of the original plan, although Helena expressed misgivings about that as well.

"I don't think he'll want to see anyone from his old crowd in Venice. Too many unpleasant memories. His last years there were so unnecessarily difficult."

Helena never had much sympathy for Walter. As far as she was concerned, his troubles in Venice were mostly self-inflicted, the result of stupid pride. "Walter is a self-made refugee," Helena had declared when Nerina first alluded to his growing desperation in Venice. "No one is forcing him to stay here. Unlike most people in the world, he's free to go anywhere he chooses."

Nerina is pleased to be able to tell Helena she's wrong to think Walter wants to avoid her. "When I spoke to him on the phone, he seemed particularly pleased to hear that you were coming." This is true enough, but she suspects that Walter's eagerness to see Helena is motivated by a desire to show off the new life he has made for himself, knowing that she will spread the word among the members of his former circle.

While Helena sleeps peacefully in the back seat, Christophe whispers to Nerina that he doesn't really mind about their trip being cut short. He's as much in a hurry as Helena to get back to Montreal and his work. And in case she thinks he has forgotten about her, he tells her that he's given some thought to how she can occupy herself while he works.

"You'll enjoy having the extra time to discover the city. Montreal is a great city to explore, particularly on foot. Not unlike Manhattan in that way, and filled with historic sites. The lack of prosperity for many years slowed the pace of development, leaving some of the older parts of the city more or less intact. It's as diverse as any other major city, but its unique French element sets it apart."

"I know. You sound like the guidebook I've been reading," she tells him, interrupting his pitch. The nervousness he is feeling about the upcoming show seems to have become generalized. "No need to sell me on the charms of the city. I wasn't all that keen on spending time in the Adirondacks."

The rain steadily intensifies as they head north. Looking out the window at the desolate landscape beneath a low-hanging, leaden sky, she feels that if it weren't for her desire to see Walter again — their meeting in Manhattan had been all too brief — she'd just as soon pass on Smith Falls and its surroundings.

Walter, sounded totally content with his life when she called to tell him she was coming. She teased him about having grown complacent in her absence, but he didn't seem to mind. "What can I say? Smith Falls has been good to me. I'll tell you all about it when I see you."

Before hanging up, he had told her that the Grand Union where she'd worked had closed down. "The recession has hit this area pretty hard," he'd said. When she inquired about Doris, Walter said he didn't know what she was doing. "Luckily her husband still has his job as a prison guard, but who knows for how long? They're talking of closing some of the prisons around here to offset the budget deficit in Albany."

"Sounds grim," Nerina said, thinking of Doris's daughter, Stacey, condemned more than ever now to her little stool and her dangerous pupils.

"The people here are used to hard times," Walter said, unperturbed. "They're resilient, like you."

She wonders what's been going on in Walter's life to account for this optimism. Perhaps it has something to do with his mysterious business trip to the city. It won't be long now before they reach his place. Walter will be able to answer her questions then.

"How are you doing?" Christophe asks, catching sight of Helena in his rear view mirror. She's been awake for some time now, but unusually silent.

"I think I'm mesmerized by the monotony of the scenery. All these vast, empty spaces, and a horizon that stretches as far as the eye can see. So different from the Italian countryside, where every inch of arable land is carefully toiled and densely populated."

"I know, the contrast is startling," Nerina agrees. "Walter says that the area is steadily losing population, and much of the farmland has reverted to wilderness. On our drives, Walter often pointed out the ruins of grand summer homes and hotels, remnants of a time when this region was a popular destination for people escaping crowded cities."

"Hard to believe," Helena says, peering through the rain-spattered window. "No wonder you sounded so desperate in your letters. What a strange place for Walter to end up after his long love affair with Venice. You could scarcely think of two places more dissimilar."

"Actually, he's quite happy living here. I think you'll be surprised to find how well the place suits him."

The rain stops when they reach Lake Placid. The sun emerges a few minutes later, transforming the gloomy landscape into a shimmering display of fall colours. As they turn onto the road leading to Walter's house, Nerina thinks of the first time she drove down it with Walter. "Welcome to America," he'd said, and the surprising formality of his words had left her on the verge of tears.

"I had forgotten how the air always smells of balsam fir here," he had observed while they lingered outdoors. "Quite a change from the stench of the canals in Venice." Sweeping his hand across the panorama of the distant mountain peaks encircling them, he turned to her and asked, "Isn't it beautiful up here?" willing her to see what he saw.

It had been the same time of year then, with the same brilliant colours all around her, but the sense of remoteness from everything she'd ever known made it difficult for her to respond.

Sensing her apprehension, Walter had put his arm around her and said, "Everything is going to work out just fine, you'll see."

Now, all this time later, she is ready to tell him he'd been right.

XXIII

Walter's find

When they turn into the driveway leading to the house they see Walter walking towards them, accompanied by two dogs.

"Don't worry, I'll put them in the barn," he tells Nerina as soon as she disembarks from the car.

"It's all right. I'm not so scared of dogs anymore," she replies, with a hint of pride.

"That's good, because they're certainly interested in you." Walter watches the dogs circle Nerina, their sensitive noses probing her clothing.

It must be Edward's scent they're picking up, she thinks, pushing them gently away.

"Well, Walter, I don't think I would have recognized you if we passed each other on the street," Helena says when they're seated in the living room.

Nerina is used to the way Walter dresses in the country — his woodsman disguise — but she, too, finds he's changed since their brief meeting in the city. For one thing he's put on some weight, and there's an air of solidity and confidence about him that wasn't there before.

The room, her old classroom, where she spent so many hours with Walter's grandfather's books, memorizing unfamiliar words and phrases, has changed as well. A fresh coat of paint, new lighting and the addition of comfortable armchairs have given the draughty space a feeling of cosiness.

"I've been fixing the old place up," he says, following her gaze. "I plan to tackle the upstairs next."

"I guess the antique business has picked up since I left."

"You could say that." He gives her an enigmatic grin. "Let me just see to the food and then I'll tell you all about it."

There's soup and smoked trout, and Walter has even managed to find bread that doesn't come out of a plastic bag. Nerina is glad now that Helena refused to stop at any of the fast food places they'd passed, except to use the washrooms.

"Do you remember my taking you to visit the Robert Louis Stevenson cottage?" Walter asks Nerina, when they're all seated around the dining room table.

"A small white cabin in Saranac Lake? Yes, I think I remember," she says, concentrating on the food. Her last meal was the breakfast she shared with Christophe at the Greek diner near his place and she's ravenous.

"Did Stevenson come here?" Helena asks. "I knew he led a wandering life, ending up in Samoa, I think — about as far from Scotland as one could get — but what brought him this far north?"

"Ill health. He was in New York City, on his way to Colorado Springs to seek treatment for tuberculosis, when he heard promising reports about a new sanatorium in Saranac Lake. On the spur of the moment, he decided to try the facility closer at hand. Not only did his health improve, but during the few months he spent here — from the fall of 1887 until April 1888 — Stevenson produced a dozen new essays and part of a new novel."

"Those Victorians were really prolific," Christophe says, sounding a little disheartened. Nerina guesses he's probably worried about the slow progress of his own work and reaches for his hand under the table.

"And remember, they did it all without computers," Helena adds with a note of satisfaction. Since being told of some nasty comments posted on a blog by one of her former protégés — a disgruntled artist who felt she hadn't done enough for him — she has considered the Internet the work of the devil.

"Does this have anything to do with the good news you alluded to on the phone?" Nerina asks. Having appeased her hunger, she is eager to hear the explanation Walter promised.

"I'm coming to that," he says, enjoying her impatience. "But first you need a little more background information. Stevenson's travelling party consisted of his wife, his stepson, his mother and the family's maid, Valentine Roch. Apart from Stevenson's mention of her in some of his letters, there isn't a great deal of information about her. But she plays an important part, in the story I'm about to tell you."

Nerina knows from experience there is no point hurrying

Walter along in his account. The slow and methodical way he proceeds when telling a story he likes does not respond to hints of edginess from his audience, and must be allowed to run its inexorable course.

"A few months ago, I purchased a couple of trunks at an estate sale," Walter continues. "One of them was filled with neat bundles of yellowing sheets of paper covered in writing. At first glance, I assumed they were letters, or someone's diary. When I began to read the pages, I realized this was a more ambitious sort of writing. Certain passages were even vaguely familiar in a way that made me think of Stevenson, whose books I had greatly admired as a boy. What's more, the dates at the top of certain pages coincided with his sojourn in this region.

"To check out my hunch, I turned to the work he'd produced during that period, including the unfinished novel *The Master of Ballantrae* — not his greatest work, I discovered. Still, despite significant differences between the printed versions and the handwritten pages, I found sufficient similarities to make me think I was on the right track. What I had stumbled upon, I concluded, were pages from earlier drafts of the books he worked on during his convalescence.

"The next step was to seek confirmation from specialists in the field. I scanned a selection of pages and sent them off to several scholars whose names I'd tracked down through the Internet. None of the scholars I contacted were ready to commit themselves on the basis of the sample pages I sent; nevertheless, they were sufficiently intrigued to encourage me to pursue the matter further."

"This is all terribly exciting," Helena interrupts. "But we still have a long drive ahead of us. Please tell us how the story ends."

"There really isn't much more to tell. Once the papers were authenticated — a fascinating story, but I'll skip the details for the sake of brevity — I sent them to Christie's to be auctioned off. That was the reason for my visit to the city, by the way," he adds, turning to Nerina, "an appointment at their offices in Rockefeller Plaza. I was told they expected the find to fetch a high price, and they were not wrong. You see, more than half of Stevenson's manuscripts have been lost as a result of his frequent moves. Those papers are now in the Yale Beinecke Library."

"Any idea how these came to be preserved?" Nerina asks, annoyed with Helena's brusqueness. After the months of humiliation he endured in Venice, Walter is entitled to relish his moment of triumph — at his own pace.

"Not really, but I've developed my own theory. The dates marked on the manuscript are all in French — *le quinze décembre*, for example. What's more, they are written in a different hand than the pages themselves. Even the ink doesn't match. This is where Valentine Roch, the family maid, comes in. According to most accounts she was either French or Swiss. In any case, she was the only one in the Stevenson household who would have noted the dates in French. I believe she saved the pages that Stevenson discarded, and before the family left the area for California and the South Seas she deposited them for safekeeping with someone she'd met during her stay here. I don't know why she kept her master's writing, or why it was never retrieved, but I intend to find out more about Valentine Roch and perhaps get some answers. Who knows, there may be a book in this."

"This is wonderful, Walter," Nerina exclaims. "You were right to believe this place would be good for you. What a great start to your new life."

"Frankly Walter, I didn't think you had it in you," Helena says. "Back in Venice, I could see nothing but failure in your future."

"Good for you, man," Christophe interrupts. "Just goes to show you can always turn things around."

Nerina gives him a grateful smile. Christophe's encouraging words have managed to offset the sting of Helena's grudging response.

"Stevenson had something interesting to say about turning your life around," Walter continues, addressing Christophe. "He wrote, 'Life is not a matter of holding good cards, but of playing a poor hand well.' I wish I'd learned that lesson earlier in life."

Helena's peevishness, however, has not run its course yet. "Not to take anything away from you Walter, but your change of fortune has more to do with dumb luck than skill," she says, regretting her words immediately. How small-minded she must seem to Nerina and Christophe. Perhaps there's still time to make amends.

"You may be right, Helena," Walter replies, before she can think of a way to soften her comments. "But at least I had the good sense to get out of Venice before it was too late. Maybe you should give some thought to doing the same. Those five flights of stairs can't be getting any easier at your age."

This is not going to end well, Nerina thinks, seeing Walter's face flush with irritation. The only way to prevent further unpleasantness, she decides, is to put a stop to their visit.

"It's been wonderful, Walter, but we really should get going," she says, rising from the table.

Christophe is ready to accompany her, but Helena seems to be finding it difficult to get to her feet. Nerina hesitates, remembering her dislike of unasked assistance, only to find that Walter has beaten her to it.

"You're right, Walter," Helena says, allowing him to help her to her feet. "The damp air of Venice and its numerous staircases can't be good for my arthritis. At my age, however, it's best not to contemplate any drastic moves."

PART FOUR

Montreal

XXIV

Gypsy blood

Nerina can't remember when she last had this much free time on her hands.

Each morning, after Christophe's early departure for the gallery, she lingers in bed taking pleasure in her unusual idleness. The sound of the chambermaid's activity in the adjacent room is her signal to dress quickly and head out. She ignores Christophe's many suggestions of interesting destinations, as well as the tourist guides available in the hotel lobby, preferring to stroll aimlessly, wherever she likes, for as long as she likes.

The city lends itself to purposeless wandering, each random direction revealing its own unexpected reward. A glimpse of a cargo ship, framed between two buildings, as it sails down the river; a narrow street opening suddenly, like a secret passageway, onto an accommodating, elegant square; spiral staircases dangling from buildings like twisted silver ribbons.

The hotel is in the old part of town, a city within the city. Its tight cobbled streets and lanes remind her of places she's known, and yet they are unlike any of them. The setting, with its large, majestic river and spacious skies, seems to her unmistakeably North American.

In time she starts to explore further afield, choosing buses rather than the metro so that she can see the sights along the way. But when Christophe asks her in the evening where she's been, she can't name any streets or landmarks, only a café where she stopped for lunch, a little shop where she bought a pair of sheepskin gloves to keep her hands warm, a place selling handmade soaps that she bought to replace the hygienic spray dispenser the hotel favours.

The people she meets are friendly, and they encourage her when she tries out her schoolgirl French. But she has no desire to allow anyone to intrude on her solitude. Unlike the loneliness brought on by the isolation of Smith Falls, to be alone and purposeless in a strange city, where she knows no one, fills her with a sense of exhilarating freedom.

Her wanderings please Christophe as well, leaving him free to concentrate on his exhibition. As for Helena, she is nearly as busy as Christophe, filling her days by visiting galleries and renewing her contacts with the many people she knows in Montreal. To Nerina's surprise, she has even set aside her objections to staying in other people's homes and accepted an invitation from Lillian Rayner, a woman she's known for years.

"Lillian is one of the most influential art patrons around," Helena said, explaining her change of policy. "I wouldn't say we're friends, but our paths have crossed many times over the years at various international art shows. Despite her reputation for being imperious and difficult, we've always gotten along reasonably well." It is Helena's hope that she can persuade Lillian to host a reception for Christophe following his opening, the way the Ohstroms did in Venice. "Her patronage could be very beneficial for Christophe," she added.

"That would be a coup," Christophe said, when Nerina repeated the conversation to him. Rémi Blois, the gallery owner, has mentioned her to him. Apparently, Rémi has been chasing after her for years.

Two days later, while they're eating Szechwan takeout in their room, Christophe tells Nerina that Helena and her friend came by the gallery that afternoon.

"I couldn't really tell what they thought of the work," Christophe says between mouthfuls of crispy chicken. "Rémi was dancing around them the whole time, so it was hard for anyone else to get a word in. I guess I should be glad he's such an enthusiastic salesman, but I would have liked to have a chance to explain my work to them myself."

"Leave it to Helena," Nerina tells him, looking for a way to end his fretting — for her own sake as well as his. "You know she has a soft spot for you, and she can be incredibly resourceful when motivated. I'm sure she'll find a way to bring you and this woman together without Rémi."

It's not long before Nerina learns her confidence in Helena was not misplaced. This time they are sharing food from a nearby Lebanese restaurant, as Christophe reports on the lunch he had earlier that day with Helena and Lillian. From the picky way he's eating, removing every shred of green pepper from his fattoush salad, she suspects the meeting did not go as well as he would have liked.

"It was a pretty tense meal," he admits. "Lillian asked a lot of tough questions about the work. I did my best to answer, but she was so impatient I found myself cut off before I could finish a sentence. Sort of like being grilled by the Grand Inquisitor."

"Probably nothing to do with you," Nerina says, trying to be supportive. But the words, emerging from the depth of her newfound tranquillity, come out sounding distant, removed.

"I guess all I do is complain these days," he says, interpreting her tone as indifference. "You must be sick of it."

"Don't worry. You still have a little credit left with me. Anyway, I intend to make you pay for your gloomy ways down the line."

"Fair enough. In the meantime, can I tell you how I disgraced myself, knocking over my glass of wine and watching it land on the ladies?"

"I hope it was white," she says, kissing him to cut off any further words of self-flagellation.

Christophe appears much more upbeat the next evening. "Let's go out tonight," he says, as soon as he enters their room. "I think we've just about completed our survey of takeouts in the area."

They choose a French restaurant recommended by Rémi. At this early hour they have the place nearly to themselves. An attentive waiter appears almost instantly and begins to recite the day's long list of specials, but Christophe cuts him off and asks him to come back later.

"What's up?" Nerina asks, surprised. "You were in such a hurry to get here, I didn't even have time to change."

He dodges her question with one of his own. "How do you like what you've seen of Montreal so far?"

The question puzzles her. She's shared her impressions of the city with him faithfully every night. And it's not as if anything eventful occurred today to change her opinion one way or the other.

"Are you ok? You're acting a little crazy you know."

"Yeah, I guess. I feel a little crazy. Tell me this, what would you say to spending a year here, maybe longer?" He leans forward, his body language conveying an intensity of interest in her response that belies his casual tone.

"Somehow I have a feeling this is not a hypothetical question, is it?"

"You're right, it's not," he admits with a smile. "I have an ulterior motive for asking it. Don't look so suspicious, Nerina, it's good news. I've been offered a teaching job at UQAM, the Université du Québec à Montréal."

He waits for her to respond, but continues when she says nothing. "One of the guys who was in art school with me is now the acting chair of the Visual Arts Department. He told me a teaching position has opened up there and he would like me to consider it. I have to admit, it's very tempting."

Nerina wishes she'd had a chance to order a glass of wine before Christophe chased the waiter away. Christophe's news has made her feel forlorn, reminding her that she doesn't know a soul in this city and that no one is chasing after her with offers of any kind.

"You're going to take it, right?" she says, trying to sound neutral.

"As I said, it's very tempting. The teaching load isn't heavy and the salary is decent. It would give me some security and I'd still have time to do my own work."

She can tell he's made up his mind, but she tries anyway. "What about New York?" she asks. "I thought you had your heart set on finding a way to stay in the city."

As she suspected, Christophe's heart has moved on. "The truth is, it's been rough going since my grant ended," he says. "I don't know how much longer I can hold on. And Rémi has an exchange deal with a gallery in New York to exhibit each other's artists. If he decides to take me on, I'd be further ahead than I am right now."

Nerina can see the attraction of this opportunity for Christophe. It would also be a return to a place to which he is connected through family history — a far cry from her own situation. She likes what she's seen of the city so far, but that's a long way from being able to conjure up a life for herself here. How many times can she bring herself to start over from scratch, without a clue of what's to come?

"What about you?" Christophe asks. "Would you find it hard to leave New York?"

She thinks about what New York means to her: Leo, Meredith, her walks with Edward, her room with the green snake coiling down the armoire. Without Christophe, there's really not much to keep her there. She sees herself perched as lightly as a bird and able to take off just as easily.

Nevertheless, she hesitates. Is it because the other times she moved it was her choice alone? Even with Walter it was she who had been the precipitating factor for their move. Walter has told her several times that, if not for his desire to help her get to America, he might have never found the courage to dislodge himself.

"I don't know," she says, trying to buy time. "This is all very sudden. I'll have to think about it."

"I understand. But let me just add one more bit of information for you to consider. I'm pretty sure Rémi can help you find a job. With your experience working for Meredith and Leo and his contacts, it shouldn't be too difficult."

"Ok. I said I'd think about it. But first, see if you can catch the waiter's attention. I think much better after I've been fed."

The next morning brings no greater clarity. As soon as Christophe leaves for the gallery, Nerina calls Marco. Who better than Marco to understand the queasy sensation of being set adrift once again? Still, she's surprised how happy she is to hear his voice when he answers.

But Marco, has only legal problems on his mind. "When are you coming back?" he asks. "The deportation hearing is still pending, but it could come up any day."

"Don't you remember? I gave a sworn statement to your lawyer before I left."

"Right, but I wish you were here. What's it like up there, by the way? If this goes badly for me, I may turn up in Canada as a refugee."

"What about Sarah and the baby? For their sake, I hope it won't come to that. Montreal is pretty nice actually. I'm thinking of trying it for a while."

"What? Just like that?" Marco's sharp tone indicates she has his full attention now. "What about your job and everything else? I bet it's that guy you've been seeing. The artist. You know, Nerina, it's never a good idea to follow a man. You could find yourself stranded in a strange city without a friend."

This advice, coming from Marco, makes her laugh. "Not all men are as unreliable as you are, you know. Anyway, I haven't made up my mind yet. And if I do decide to stay, it will be because I've found something that interests me, something that will make my life better, and not just because of Christophe. You're not the only one with ambition, you know."

"You're up to something, aren't you?" Marco says, suddenly suspicious. Although vague about his own activities, it annoys him when he suspects Nerina is holding out on him. "Want to try it out on me?"

She doesn't. What she's been thinking about since her conversation with Christophe last night feels more like a fantasy than a plan of action. Definitely not something she's ready to talk about just yet.

"Whatever I decide, you'll be the first to know," she tells Marco. "I promise."

Her answer seems to satisfy him. "I know what you mean

about ambition," he says. "If I manage to get out of this mess, I've made up my mind: things will be different."

She can hear conviction in his voice, but she can't resist teasing him. "That's good. You don't want your kid to have a thief for a father."

"You realize it won't be easy breaking with family tradition," he says, sounding wistful. "The Gypsy blood in our veins makes it hard to live by other people's rules."

"Try that on the immigration authorities," she says, losing patience. "Let me know how it works out for you next time we speak."

XXV
Galerie Sarajevo

Nerina's walks are no longer aimless. Equipped with the names and addresses of the Montreal galleries she found online at an Internet café, she is working her way down the list. It's all part of a plan that she hopes will bring her closer to the goal of running her own gallery in the not too distant future.

The idea, lurking at the edges of her mind for some time now, came into sharper focus when Christophe asked her to move to Montreal with him. Everything he told her about the city's thriving art scene, its cheap rents — the lowest of any city in North America — as well as what she has seen for herself in the last few days, has encouraged her to feel that she just might be able to pull it off.

The first step, she decided, was to speak to Walter. It had taken her hours to work up her nerve to call him, but in the end ambition overcame timidity.

"Sounds like a promising proposition," he'd said, after carefully listening to her reasons for requesting a loan. "And don't worry about paying me back. I'm thinking more along the lines of acting as your silent partner. I have a feeling you're a safer bet than the stock market these days. You've brought me luck so far."

Nerina doesn't put much trust in luck, but she's determined to live up to Walter's faith in her. For a start, she knows she needs further training. The bits and pieces of knowledge she's picked up from Meredith, Leo and Helena will come in handy, but what she needs is practical, hands-on experience to learn what running a gallery really entails. Finding the right place that will take her on as an apprentice, with the possibility of playing a more important role in the future, is crucial. She is determined to do it on her own, without the help of Christophe or Rémi.

She hasn't come across anything suitable so far, but she's not discouraged. The city is full of all kinds of galleries, ranging from those dealing in the work of internationally recognized artists to the modest artist-run holes in the wall. Today, she is setting out to visit several galleries in a converted industrial building in the downtown area of the city.

A couple of blocks from her destination she finds her path suddenly blocked by a noisy group of demonstrators, who are being herded by police in riot gear.

"Prince Charles and Camilla are inside the Black Watch Armoury across the street," a man on the sidelines explains when she stops to inquire. "The protesters are denouncing the presence of British Royals in Quebec. You know, *à bas la monarchie,*" he adds, making the thumbs-down sign.

She wavers for a moment, wondering if she should persist and push her way through the mob. "Any idea how long they'll be in there?" she asks.

According to her informant, the Royals are on a hit-and-run schedule that does not allow for lingering at any of the stops on their daylong itinerary. "A fast-moving target is harder to hit," he concludes with a grin.

Nerina knows he's kidding, but she decides to walk in the opposite direction, away from the angry voices. The visit she'd planned can wait until things have quieted down.

A half hour later, she finds herself on a narrow cobblestoned street lined with ethnic restaurants and small, cheerful-looking shops. The street seems vaguely familiar; she thinks she may have passed here before, but this time her eyes are drawn to a sign she's sure she's never seen: Galerie Sarajevo.

She presses the doorbell and is buzzed in to a long room lined with paintings. Beyond it, she catches a glimpse of a workshop with tables and a display of frame samples on the walls. A woman with long, greying hair, dressed in denim overalls, comes out of the back room to greet her.

"We're not really open right now," she says, speaking English with a strong French accent. "But you're welcome to look around if you like."

Nerina makes a note to add another crucial item to her to-do list: start learning French.

"I'm curious about the name of your place," she says. "I was passing by and it sort of pulled me in."

"It happens a lot, people dropping in looking for some

connection. The truth is there's none. When I opened this place in the early nineties, Sarajevo was much in the news. Terrible stories. It was my way of expressing solidarity with the besieged city. Turned out to be a lucky choice for me. I'm still here."

It crosses Nerina's mind that if she were to link up with the gallery, its name would no longer be merely symbolic. But she's getting ahead of herself.

"I see that you have a framing workshop behind the gallery," she says, trying to sound calmer than she feels. "I work in a similar kind of place in New York. Samuels' Framers?"

"I've seen the name, but I don't get to travel much. This place keeps me very busy."

She starts to walk away and Nerina can't think of a way to stop her. But the woman changes her mind and turns back to Nerina.

"I was just about to send out for coffee. Why don't you join me, if you have time? I'd be interested to hear more about the place where you work. My name is Claire," she adds, extending her hand.

While they wait for the coffee, Nerina switches the conversation back to Galerie Sarajevo. "You mentioned that you started this gallery. How did it come about?"

"It sort of happened by accident," Claire says, pulling out a chair for Nerina while she resumes work on a metal frame on the table. "I was living with an artist at the time and I started out making frames for him and some of his friends. I was always good with my hands and I learned a lot from my *papa*. He was a cabinetmaker, you know. The artists talked about needing a place to show their work, and so I suggested we form a *coopérative*. A workshop for me and an exhibition space up front. The arrangement didn't last very long. My boyfriend and I split up and he moved on. The other artists drifted away as well, and I soon found myself running the whole show on my own."

"You must have done all right, seeing how long you've lasted," Nerina says, hoping she's not being too intrusive.

"It was hard going at first," Claire replies, without any hesitation. "If I hadn't had the framing business to fall back on, I probably wouldn't be here now. It takes time and *persistance* to spot new talent and build up a client list. Once the artists become established, you must work even harder to hold on to them. It's a cut-throat business — *sauvage au bout* — and it's all-consuming."

None of this is news to Nerina, and it sounds as if Claire could use some help. "Do you do all this on your own?" she asks, encouraged by Claire's candour.

"I have someone to help with the frames, but it's not easy to find people willing to work for what I can afford to pay. To tell you the truth I feel like I'm headed for a bad case of burnout. Not sure how much longer I can carry on this way."

Nerina can scarcely believe how easily her plan is falling into place. All that remains is to convince Claire.

"This may be your lucky day," she says, feeling that all the luck is on her side. "Let me help. I have some experience and I need a job. You see, I'm planning to move to Montreal shortly, and I don't really know anyone here. This could be great for both of us. I have to find work and you need help."

"Are you serious?" Claire asks, taken aback by Nerina's outburst. "I don't think you understand my situation. What I can offer in the way of a salary wouldn't be enough for you to live on."

"Let me worry about that," Nerina says, dismissing Claire's objection. "All I really want is a chance to learn everything I can about running a place like this. Who knows, if things work out, we could be partners down the line," she adds, unable stop herself.

"Why me?" Claire asks, looking puzzled. "There are more successful galleries in town. Wouldn't it make more sense to start at the top?"

"Not for me," Nerina insists. "Yours is the sort of place I'd like to have one day. The kind that shows young artists before they're well known. And I like that you have the framing as backup insurance."

"I don't know," Claire says, searching Nerina's face for a clue to her enthusiasm. "Maybe you should give it some more thought."

Nerina decides to throw the last piece of the puzzle into the mix. "Would it make more sense if I told you I was born in Sarajevo? You could say it was preordained that I would find my way to your place."

She laughs to indicate she doesn't really believe what she just said, but Claire takes her seriously.

"What's meant to be will always find a way," she says.

"Is that you, or some great philosopher?" Nerina asks, pleased to see the look of suspicion on Claire's face has given way to a smile.

"Tricia Yearwood. My favourite country and western artist," Claire says. Coming out from behind the table she takes hold of Nerina's hand. "All right, I'll give it some serious thought. Come by tomorrow and we'll talk some more. We'll soon find out if it's meant to be or not."

Maybe Claire and this Yearwood woman are on to something, Nerina wonders after leaving the gallery. If Prince Charles and Camilla hadn't been in town this day, and if a group of protesters hadn't gathered to demonstrate against their presence in Quebec, she might have never stumbled onto Claire's place. She had missed it somehow when compiling her list of galleries.

But she can't really see what has just taken place as anything more than a fortuitous sequence of events. The haphazard way things happen in life — anybody's life — may be a source of wonder, but it's no reason to bring in the heavy hand of fate.

XXVI

A reason for everything

Nerina spends an anxious night worrying that she's ruined her chances with Claire. The sense of elation she'd felt when she left Galerie Sarajevo has worn off, to be replaced by dismay and self-recrimination as she reviews her behaviour. Why had she been in such a hurry to blurt out her intentions to a total stranger? Why hadn't she been more restrained and allowed more time for the two of them to get to know each other before throwing herself at Claire? Claire must have found her pathetically desperate, or even unhinged. Definitely not collaborator material.

When she turns up for her appointment at Galerie Sarajevo the next day, she finds that Claire has also been thinking about their meeting, and seems eager to pick up their conversation where it left off.

"I believe things happen for a reason," she says, addressing Nerina in a sober tone softened by an encouraging smile. "I don't know if you agree with me, but I don't think there are any accidents in life."

Nerina feels this is nonsense — what good reason could there have been for the smash-up that killed her parents, or the mortar shells and sniper bullets that terrorized her native city for four years? Right now, she doesn't care how simpleminded Claire's beliefs are as long as they work in her favour.

And it looks as if they do.

"I've been thinking about your proposal," Claire continues. "If you still want to work here for what little I can pay you, I'm prepared to take you on and I'll try and teach you what I know. Time will tell which one of us is getting the better part of the bargain. In the meantime, we'll take it a day at a time."

"Thank you," Nerina says, restraining herself from hugging Claire. "You have no idea what this means to me. I was afraid I'd put you off yesterday with my enthusiasm."

"Don't worry about it. I tend to trust intuition more than words and I have a good feeling about you. I think we're going to get along just fine."

Nerina leaves the gallery in a state of pleasant agitation, but her thoughts soon turn towards Leo. Now that Claire has agreed to take her on as an apprentice, she feels she should warn him as soon as possible of her upcoming departure. He'll need time to find her replacement.

"How's your mother?" she asks, before launching into her big news.

"Not good," Leo says, sounding discouraged. "She's back in the hospital with a fever. Some sort of infection. The doctors are hoping to do the surgery as soon as the fever goes down."

"You mean she's agreed to have the operation?" Perhaps Leo was right about Helena being a bad influence.

"Right now she's too sick to make any decisions. But the rabbi from her synagogue has been talking to her, and I think his message is sinking in."

"What has he said that's making a difference?" Nerina interrupts, curious to know what would change Miriam's mind after all her resistance.

"The rabbi has simply reminded her that according to Jewish Law the saving of a life, including your own, is paramount. Instead of relying on prayers or miracles, Jews are encouraged to seek out medical treatment. She trusts her rabbi, so I'm hopeful. In the meantime, I'd appreciate it if you didn't say anything to Helena, just in case she takes a notion to rush back."

"Of course not," Nerina assures him.

Maybe now is not the best time to tell him she won't be coming back, but she doesn't want to leave him in the lurch the way her predecessor had.

Leo, seems to welcome the change of subject, and takes her news in stride.

"I had a feeling you'd be moving on one of these days," he says, when she pauses for his reaction. "You've got brains, ambition and a talent for handling artists. I saw how quickly you made yourself indispensable to Meredith as well as in the shop. Now tell me what attracts you to this setup in Montreal."

She starts to describe Galerie Sarajevo, but after only a few words Leo interrupts her to respond to an incoming call. "Have to take this. It's the hospital," he says.

When the phone rings a few minutes later, she assumes it's Leo calling back. "Everything all right?" she asks.

But the voice that answers is Helena's. "Who knows? I've just called Columbia-Presbyterian to find out how Miriam is doing but they won't tell me a thing."

Nerina is dumbfounded for a moment. "What made you think she was there?" she asks, unable to conceal her surprise.

"I kept calling her apartment, and finally her cleaning woman answered. She told me Miriam was in the hospital. Do you know anything about this?" Helena asks, sounding suspicious.

"Just heard about it from Leo," she says, feeling there is no point in keeping her promise to him now.

"I called him as well, but got nothing out of him. As bad as the hospital. I guess this means she's finally decided to have the surgery." Helena pauses, waiting for confirmation from Nerina.

"I don't know. We didn't talk very long." Somehow, she doesn't think Helena will be pleased to hear that Miriam is more receptive to her rabbi than to her long-lost cousin.

"Well, let's hope for the best. I feel sort of responsible, since I really pushed her hard to have the surgery. Nothing I can do about that now, I'm afraid."

Nerina would like to ease Helena's mind by telling her the real reason Miriam is back in the hospital, but that would mean betraying what's left of her promise to Leo.

Much better just to change the subject, but she can think of only one way to divert Helena's attention away from Leo and his mother. "Can I run something by you, Helena?" she asks. "I need your advice. I'm thinking of going into the art business."

"Really?" Helena's voice is tinged with sarcasm. "Have you suddenly acquired talents I don't know about? Why is it that everyone I meet these days seems to think he or she can become an artist?"

"Relax," Nerina says, laughing. "You've got it wrong. I want to work with artists, not be one."

"A recipe for heartbreak, either way," Helena says. "But all right, you may as well tell me all about it."

Nerina would have preferred to set out her plan in person; now, she has no choice but to finish what she's started.

"You've come a long way from sweeping floors at Lorenzo's salon," Helena says, when Nerina finishes. "Even back then, I suspected there was more to you than met the eye."

So far, so good, Nerina thinks, but she knows Helena is not done with her yet. "I'm so glad I haven't disappointed you," she quickly interrupts, hoping to stave off the criticism she feels is coming.

Helena ignores the interruption and calmly continues. "I wish you the best of luck, my dear. But it would be remiss of me not to warn you that you're getting yourself into a very risky business. You have a better chance betting on horses than on artists. At least horses respond to the whip."

"Thanks, Helena," Nerina says, eager to end the conversation. "I knew I could count on you to set me straight."

XXVII

Selling yourself

Christophe is late getting back from the gallery — no surprise — and as she waits for him in their hotel room, Nerina keeps thinking about Helena's cautionary words. They haven't dampened her interest in Galerie Sarajevo, but they have made her uncomfortably aware that the money she is risking is not her own.

She decides to call Walter, feeling it's only fair to let him know about Helena's negative reaction to her plan.

"Never mind," Walter says when she's finished. "By the time you're ready to buy into the business, you'll have spent several months working at the gallery. That should give you a pretty good idea of how well it's doing. And if that place doesn't work out, you can look around for a better deal. Anyway, the money is here for you, to use when you need it."

"I appreciate your support, Walter. I'm really starting to have butterflies about the whole thing." She finds herself confessing her worries to Walter more readily than to anyone else. It's a habit that dates back to the days in Venice when he used to listen patiently while she tried to convey, in her few words of English, her frustrations with immigration authorities.

"Maybe it will help if I tell you that Helena's view is tainted by a bad experience she had years ago, when she was first married," Walter says. "Her husband ran a gallery that soon went bankrupt, and Helena found herself pursued by his creditors. The husband had disappeared by this time. Rumour had it he ran the business into the ground with his extravagant ways. But that's not your problem. I still remember how well you managed on next to nothing in Venice. Nerina, I have faith in you."

Walter's words are encouraging, but she doubts his explanation of Helena's motives. Helena's caution is based on a lifetime of experience in the fickle ways of the art business, not just on a single, long-ago misfortune. The truth is that Walter and Helena never miss a chance to disparage one another and there is little she can do to change that.

Fortunately, Christophe and Helena are on excellent terms. It helps that Helena has spared no effort on his behalf, including her latest coup: persuading Lillian Rayner to host a reception following his opening. Christophe doesn't know about it yet, and Nerina is planning to surprise him with the news tonight — that is, if he ever gets back.

As for her own news, she's in no hurry to share it with Christophe. In the midst of his work-induced craziness, the question of her joining him in Montreal is not uppermost in his mind. For the time being she's been put on the back burner, but she knows her turn will come. She will inform him of her decision then, once she has his full attention.

She dozes off at the hotel while waiting for Christophe. When he finally arrives, she can tell from the speed with which he strips off his tee shirt and jeans that he has not had a good day. They have not been together long, but already Nerina is familiar with the signs that indicate his varying moods. The need to shed his clothes after a day in the gallery — socks and underwear included — is a sure symptom of distress.

Half asleep, she watches Christophe, naked, examine the contents of the sparse wardrobe he's brought along with him. She considers luring him into bed, but she can tell he's feeling miserable, not sexy.

"What's wrong?" she asks, although she's pretty sure the answer has something to do with Rémi. She hasn't met him yet, but ever since Christophe started working with him his feelings have swung between gratitude towards the man for giving him a show and irritation with his constant, interfering presence. Either way, Rémi is never far from Christophe's thoughts these days.

She's pretty sick of hearing about Rémi, but knows the surest way to improve Christophe's mood is to encourage him to vent his frustrations.

"Come on, talk to me. What's got you so riled up tonight?"

"More of the same, another wasted day," he says, settling on a pair of jeans and a black tee shirt indistinguishable from those he's just discarded. "Rémi's clients kept dropping in all day, no doubt invited by him for a sneak preview, even though I told him I didn't want anyone around until the whole show was installed. It's his way of making them feel special. What's more, he expected me to stop what I was doing and talk about my work with each new arrival. More accurately, he wanted me to amuse them as he does. You should see the way he courts these people, flattering them shamelessly. He's really good at what he does. I just wish he'd leave me out of it."

"Never mind," Nerina says, filing away his complaint for future dealings with artists. "Just think how happy you'll be when his annoying ways result in sales. I'm sure Rémi knows what he's doing. You were the one who told me his gallery is one of the most respected in town."

"I know," he says, tugging at his clothes as if they were the source of his misery. "It's just that I'm nervous about how the show will be received, and having people around, judging the work before it's even up, doesn't help."

"Come over here," Nerina says, tapping the place beside her on the bed. "What you need is a nap."

She can feel the tension in his body as he lies stiffly next to her. It's been days since he's made any attempt to touch her. Back in New York, Christophe had talked about how great it would be to finally share a room together. But with the exhibition opening only days away, Christophe, like an athlete before a big competition, has been conserving his sexual energy for his work.

Feeling like Delilah about to sap Samson's strength, she presses herself against him and begins gently to caress him. It doesn't take long for his body to respond, gratefully, to the attention it's receiving. "God, that feels good," he murmurs between sighs of pleasure.

"Welcome back from the dead. For a while there, I wasn't sure I could bring you around."

"You should know what it's like preparing for a show after working for Meredith," he says, with a hint of reproach.

"Yes, but I wasn't fucking Meredith."

Christophe laughs, looking relaxed for the first time since he came back. "Fair enough. Come on, I'm starving. Let's get something to eat," he says, bounding out of bed with new energy.

Later, while they're waiting for their food in an Indian restaurant near the hotel, she remembers that she hasn't told him Helena's good news. She suspects it will make him even happier than the sex they just had, but she doesn't mind. She'd be a hypocrite to hold his ambition against him.

Christophe's face lights up with pleasure when she tells him about the party Lillian Rayner has agreed to host in his honour. "Helena is amazing. I'll owe her big time for pulling this off. Rémi, of course, will be thrilled. He's been trying to ingratiate himself with Rayner for a long time."

"You see, everything is going to work out just fine." She likes to be the consoling one, but not so much that she'd want to make a career of it.

He gives her a grateful look and reaches across the table to take hold of her hand. "I know I've been pretty distracted lately. Will you give me the chance to make it up to you?"

Nerina suddenly feels a strong desire to tell him she's come up with a plan that should allow him endless opportunities for redeeming himself. But just as she prepares to launch into her story about Galerie Sarajevo and her arrangement with Claire, Christophe's cell phone rings.

"It's Rémi," he says, glancing at the caller display.

The conversation that follows is in rapid French; she doesn't understand what's being said, but she can see from the way Christophe's lips narrow and his shoulders stiffen that all her efforts back in the hotel room are being wiped out before her eyes.

"Tell him about Lillian Rayner," Nerina whispers, trying to help, but Christophe ignores her.

"*D'accord. Je viens*," he says, ending the conversation.

Turning to Nerina, he tells her he has to leave. "Rémi insists I meet him right away. He's in a bar not far from here, having a drink with the art critic from *Le Devoir*. Feel like coming along?"

She can tell he'd rather go alone, and in any case her French won't be good enough to follow the conversation.

"No, I think I'll just linger here and enjoy my gulab jamun."

He gives her a small smile of regret, and hurries out the door.

She feels almost sorry for him, watching him rush off for the command performance Rémi has arranged. Yet she knows that most of the artists hanging around Leo's shop would be glad for the chance to do the same, any hour of day or night. Selling yourself is part of the artist's job. As Helena puts it, "No one *needs* art. It's up to the artist to persuade the world otherwise."

"Will *monsieur* be coming back?" the waiter asks, refilling her water glass.

"Not tonight. I'll take his dessert with me. He'll enjoy it later."

Walking back to the hotel, the sticky syrup in which the gulab jamun floats starts to leak through the Styrofoam container, coating her hand. She tosses it into the first garbage can she passes. As for her sticky hand, if Christophe comes back before she's asleep, she'll let him lick it clean.

XXVIII

Life goes on

"Bad things happen, life goes on."

As Nerina makes her way through the party crowd, words drift past her like puffs of dandelion seeds, some hard to catch, others, like the sentence she's just overheard, attaching themselves to her without any effort on her part.

The remark comes from a stylishly dressed woman who's talking to Helena at the moment. Nerina slides past them, not ready to plunge into the fray. There will be time enough for that when she moves to the city and the routine of starting a new life in a new place will oblige her to be attentive and alert to her surroundings. For now, while the party swirls around her, she enjoys the feeling of being anonymous, invisible, free of all claims.

"I know you," a woman with spiky dark hair says, stopping in front of Nerina and shattering her illusion of invisibility. "You're the girl in the video!"

Nerina is surprised the woman has recognized her. The images, shot by Christophe while she slept, have been digitally altered to show only brief glimpses of her face behind wavy blue lines. When Christophe first showed her the video, she accused him — only half-jokingly — of wanting to put her behind bars.

The bars had nothing to do with her, Christophe explained. "The use of verticality superimposed on the reclining, horizontal form is an expression of the dialectic between consciousness and unconsciousness," he'd told her.

Nerina wasn't sure what he meant. As far as she was concerned, the only useful function the stripes performed was to conceal her identity.

It turns out she was wrong.

"My name is Caroline," the woman says, looking at Nerina with an appraising eye. "And you must be Christophe's new muse. I knew him years ago, you know, when he first came to Montreal. We even dated for a while."

The woman's smile is friendly, but Nerina edges away. This is not the first revelation she's heard tonight about Christophe's past. Several people at the opening, and now at Lillian Rayner's party, appear to know more about him than she does. Caroline, like the others who've shared their reminiscences with her, seems to feel this creates a bond between them.

"You must tell me all about it sometime," Nerina replies with what she hopes is an equally friendly smile, while looking around for a likely escape.

She's been smiling non-stop for hours and feels she has earned a break. The large terrace beyond the French doors of the reception room looks promising, but it turns out to be nearly as packed as the living room. Among the guests lured outdoors by the unusually mild weather is Helena, now chatting with Lillian Rayner, their hostess. Nerina hopes they're too engrossed to notice her, but no such luck.

"Come and join us," Helena calls out, waving her over. "Lillian was just telling me about the city's history." For Lillian's benefit, she adds, "Nerina is planning to move here, you know."

The news does not appear to interest Lillian, who resumes her commentary on the scene before them. "As I was saying, this is where the city began, right here, at the tip of the island. The sheltered bay, just beyond the point of convergence of two rivers, made it a natural site for a settlement. Indigenous people lived here long before Jacques Cartier landed in 1535 and claimed the land for France. The harbour is less important now, but when I was a girl, these docks and the grain elevators you see in the distance teemed with traffic. I can still remember the excitement I felt as a child the first time our family boarded one of the Cunard ocean liners bound for Southampton."

"There's nothing as grand about the Rio San Vio, the waterway I look out on every day," Helena says when Lillian pauses. "A dank, narrow canal, it accommodates only the most modest of boats. But what it reflects is unchanging and comforting. Were I to live in close proximity to the St. Lawrence, or the Hudson for that matter, it would be like looking in a mirror and seeing a stranger every time."

It makes Nerina sad to think of Helena ending her days alone in the dusty rooms above the stagnant waters of the canal. Or maybe what's making her sad is knowing how much she will miss Helena. Before she can say anything, she sees that Caroline, the woman with the spiky hair, has found her way to the terrace as well and is heading in their direction. This time she's interested in Lillian, not Nerina.

"I just had to come over and tell you what a thrill it is to see the inside of this house," she tells Lillian. "There are so few eighteenth-century houses left, especially ones as well restored and maintained as yours is."

Caroline, it turns out, is an architect. While she lists the finer points of the house that have caught her attention — its pleasing proportions, the use of reserved and delicate details, the excellent workmanship — Nerina seizes the chance to escape. It's not that she's not interested in what Caroline has to say; it's just hard for her right now to stay still long enough to listen.

What keeps her on the move is apprehension. Any conversation, no matter how innocuous at the start, soon feels like the grip of an aggressive tendril that is about to entwine her and hold her captive. This isn't a new sensation. Each one of her moves — to Venice, Smith Falls, Manhattan — was preceded by the same odd mixture of giddiness and stage fright that she feels tonight. It's all part of steeling herself to take on the hidden pitfalls that come with each new setting.

She's done it before and in more difficult circumstances, she reminds herself as she makes her way across the large reception area, now even more crowded than before. She catches sight of Christophe, talking to a small group. He doesn't notice her, but just the sight of him makes her feel better: this time, she won't be alone. Once the strain and excitement of the exhibition are behind him, Christophe will be at her side, acting as her guide. This, at least, is what she chooses to tell herself — and to believe.

A long flight of stairs takes her to the front door. She pulls it open and lights up as soon as she has one foot on the sidewalk; the other remains in the entryway to prevent the heavy door from clicking shut behind her. She doesn't want to embarrass Christophe on the night of his triumph by locking herself out or, worse, setting off the alarm system.

A moment later, Rémi Blois, Christophe's dealer, appears in the doorway, cigarette in hand. They met briefly earlier at the gallery, but he barely acknowledges her greeting.

Nerina doesn't take his coolness personally. She has watched him work the crowd and she understands he needs a break even more than she does. She is also aware that of all the people to cultivate tonight, she is the least important.

Neither one of them is pleased to see the other but at least Nerina can take advantage of his arrival to move forward, obliging Rémi to become the doorstop. The look he gives her as the heavy door slams into his ankle is even less friendly than his greeting, but she doesn't care. Rid of the burden of the door, she spins away from him into the street, relishing her moment of freedom.

The ringing of church bells suddenly fills the street and Nerina looks around to see where they're coming from.

"That's Notre-Dame-de-Bon-Secours, the oldest chapel in Montreal," Rémi volunteers, sounding a little friendlier, as he points to a church at the end of the block. "Also known as the

Sailor's Church. There is an interesting display of carved replicas of sailing ships hanging from its vault. You should go inside and check it out," he adds, giving her an encouraging smile.

"You mean right now?" she asks, scrutinizing his face to see if he's serious.

"Why not?" He looks at her slyly. "Christophe won't miss you."

This time it is personal, but for Christophe's sake Nerina holds her tongue and walks quickly back inside the house. Rémi is right behind her.

Christophe is now talking to a tall, slender woman wearing what looks like a shrunken human head on a thick, carved chain. Must be someone from the art world, Nerina guesses. Who else would have the courage to wear something so hideous?

Just to annoy Rémi, who's caught up to her, she starts out in Christophe's direction. She instantly feels the grip of Rémi's hand on her arm.

"You don't want to interrupt Christophe right now," he hisses in her ear. "That's Alessandra Berman he's talking to, head of contemporary art at the National Museum. She can be a great help to him."

"Relax," she tells him, disengaging her arm. "I have no intention of intruding." To prove that she means what she says, she wanders over to join Helena, who is standing alone.

"He's a bit of a snake, isn't he?" Helena says, as they watch Rémi talking in animated fashion to a short, heavyset man. "That's Sy Gollen, a big-time art collector," Helena tells Nerina. "The very thin woman next to him is his long-suffering wife."

Nerina recognizes the woman. She's the one whose words earlier in the evening caught her attention: "Bad things happen, life goes on."

"Why long-suffering?" Nerina asks, wondering if Helena's description has anything to do with the remark she overheard.

"Gollen is a compulsive womanizer," Helena says with an indulgent chuckle. "Rumour has it he's currently carrying on with Alessandra Berman, the woman talking to Christophe. Apparently she's persuaded him to donate his collection to the National Museum. Gollen made his fortune in real estate — shopping malls, I believe — but he has a keen appreciation for art and beautiful women. Looks like he's heading our way."

Nerina starts to back away, but Helena stops her. "I won't have you running off again. What's wrong with you tonight? You've been as restless as a hummingbird."

Helena's scolding makes her feel even less invisible than being recognized from Christophe's video. She wonders who else has noticed her skittish behaviour. For Christophe's sake, and her own, she must try and make a better impression before the party ends.

"Helena, what a delight to see you," Gollen says, kissing her hand. "I think of you fondly every time I look at the Piranesi print you advised me to buy. It was in a private collection in Venice," he says, turning towards Nerina. "Helena persuaded its owners to part with it, for a painfully high sum as I recall."

"You know as well as I do Sy, it's worth twice as much now," Helena points out. "Speaking of art purchases, I've heard you've acquired a couple of Meredith Covington's recent works. You know Nerina has been her assistant for the past year."

Gollen is only too happy to seize the opening Helena has provided. "I'd love to hear about your experiences with Meredith," he says, steering Nerina slightly to one side. "One hears so many fascinating stories about her."

"You probably know more about her than I do," Nerina replies. Aware that Helena is watching her, she adds, "I'd much rather hear about your collection. Helena says you have a very keen eye for art."

"Helena is too kind. The truth is I knew nothing about art when I started," he says, sounding pleased with his former ignorance. "Donna, my wife, was the art buyer in the family."

Remembering the resolve she just made to be more sociable, Nerina wills herself to pursue the conversation. "What changed that?" she asks.

"Donna persuaded me to accompany her to a few auctions and I caught the bug. My first purchases were of French Impressionists, but I soon switched to contemporary art. It was less expensive, and I liked the fact that it was more of a gamble. Altogether a more likely source for creating a large and original collection. Next time you're in town, I could arrange for you to see it."

"Thank you. I'd like that," Nerina replies. After a moment's hesitation, she adds, "I'm actually planning to move here in a couple of weeks."

"Excellent," Gollen responds, beaming approval. "I'm always pleased when I hear someone your age is moving to Montreal.

For a long time, it was mostly a place young people left. Have you thought about what you're going to do? This isn't New York, but the art scene here is pretty lively."

This is the perfect moment to tell him about her plans. No doubt that's why Helena has left her alone with Gollen. She knows the right tone to strike: enthusiastic, but casual, without a hint of neediness; she's learned from the Ohstroms that people like Gollen, rich people, are always on guard for any kind of solicitation.

As she starts to talk, Sy Gollen interrupts to ask where she's from. "I'm intrigued by your charming accent, which I can't quite place. Central Europe, I would guess, but which country?"

"The former Republic of Yugoslavia," she says, keeping it non-specific.

"Really? Which part? My wife and I had a great time at the Winter Olympics in Sarajevo in 1984. You probably weren't even born then."

She's looking for a way to bring the conversation back to Montreal, when she sees Alessandra hurrying towards them, the shrunken head swinging menacingly between her breasts like a weapon.

"Hi," she says brightly, slipping her arm through Gollen's as if to assert her claim.

Nerina can see that Alessandra's abrupt departure has left Christophe looking a little stunned. As for Rémi, the expression of dismay on his face strikes Nerina as comical: the two people he wanted her to stay away from have both sought her out, although for different reasons.

"Hello Alessandra," Gollen says, friendly as ever. "This is Nerina. You'll be interested to hear that she knows Meredith Covington." For Nerina's benefit he adds, "Alessandra has written a brilliant analysis of Meredith's work. Way over my head, I'm afraid."

Ignoring Nerina, Alessandra tightens her hold on Gollen's arm. "I need to speak with you," she says. "Right now."

"I'll be with you in a moment," Gollen replies in an even tone, disengaging his arm. "Nerina was just in the middle of telling me her plans for setting up a gallery in Montreal. You might find this interesting as well, Alessandra."

Alessandra, her face flushed with anger, strides off without another word.

Nerina is not sure what has just happened, but she suspects she's been used as ammunition in some struggle between Gollen and Alessandra.

"This is probably not the best time or place to talk," she says, unwilling to give Alessandra any further reason for animosity. "In any case, my plans are still pretty vague."

"All right," Gollen replies in the same even tone he used with Alessandra. "Don't forget to give me a call once you've settled in," he adds, handing her his card.

When she describes the encounter to Helena a few minutes later, Helena tells her not to worry about Alessandra. "She wouldn't like you no matter what you did. Alessandra has made her reputation as a brilliant theoretician of feminist art, but according to Lillian, who's on the board of the Museum, she can be quite cruel towards women staff members. Nor does it prevent her from poaching other women's husbands. I bet Gollen's wife, Donna, is grateful to you for bringing her down a few pegs."

Nerina doesn't feel she deserves either blame or credit for Alessandra's humiliation, but before she has a chance to protest, Lillian reappears beside them.

"How did you make out?" Helena asks her, sounding solicitous.

Helena's inquiry, it soon becomes apparent, concerns Lillian's dog. The animal suffers from digestive problems, and his vet has prescribed a twice-daily dose of Metamucil to increase his fibre intake. Not an easy remedy to administer, according to Lillian — and to Helena, who has witnessed Lillian's struggles.

"What kind of dog do you have?" Nerina asks. Lillian seems much friendlier after her ordeal than she did on the terrace earlier.

"A Bouvier des Flandres. They're intelligent, loyal dogs, but they tend to have nervous stomachs. My goodness, there he is," she says, pointing to a large, heavily furred animal standing in the doorway. "He's not supposed to come in here."

The dog, aware he's on borrowed time, scoots into the room before anyone can stop him, his progress across forbidden territory soon marked by a trail of foul odour — unmistakeable proof of his nervous stomach.

"Now, how did you get in here?" his owner asks, looking at the dog with a fondness that doesn't match her stern tone. As she grabs his collar to drag him out of the room, the dog disgraces himself further by vomiting on the parquet floor.

"How disgusting," Alessandra says, as she pushes past them to the terrace. Other guests are not far behind. Nerina finds herself swept along in the stampede and thrust against Christophe.

"How are you doing?" he asks, putting his arm around her waist to steady her.

"Are you sure you want to be seen talking to me? Rémi won't like it."

"Fuck Rémi," he says, tightening his hold of her body.

As if on cue, Rémi pops up in front of them, smiling impishly. This time, he's not here to break up their tête-à-tête but to share a rumour he's just heard, too delicious to keep to himself: the dog's troubles may be the result of an act of human mischief, not an act of nature.

"It's entirely possible, you know," Rémi says, his voice an excited whisper, as he leans in closer to emphasize the intimate nature of his disclosure. "I can think of a couple of artists here tonight who are quite capable of staging a show of excremental aesthetics. You know, like Manzoni, the Italian artist, who put his own shit in sealed cans and sold it as art from the gut. All you'd have to do is feed the beast a few of those canapés of foie gras or curried shrimp and wait for nature to take its course."

Nerina could blow his story out of the water by the mere mention of Metamucil, but Rémi is so caught up in the plot he's weaving she doesn't have the heart to spoil his fun.

"What a twisted mind you have," Christophe says, laughing. "I wouldn't put it past you to stage this *coup de théâtre* all by yourself."

The accusation brings a wistful smile to Rémi's face. "I wish I had that kind of imagination, but I don't. That's why I'm a dealer, not an artist."

A cold wind coming off the river forces the guests back inside. There is no trace left of the dog's mess or his foul odour, but the party is winding down. Lillian and Helena are nowhere to be seen, perhaps off ministering to the ailing dog, or maybe they've simply retired for the night. Only Rémi still perseveres, plying his trade among the remaining guests, as sharp and tireless as at the outset of the evening.

Nerina is ready to leave as well, but she waits patiently while Christophe takes one final lap around the room talking to the last stragglers. He is reluctant to see the evening end and she understands. So much effort leading up to this moment, and so little assurance of how it will play out.

Tonight's party, with its seamy undercurrent of greed and ambition hidden beneath the camouflage of glamour and the pursuit of beauty, casts even further doubt on Christophe's aspirations, as well as her own. The art business is not for the faint-hearted.

As she watches the waiters scurrying around the room to collect the debris of the party — it's been a long night for them as well — Nerina is suddenly struck by the vast uncertainty of it all, for Christophe, for herself, and for the others whose stories have become entangled with her own: Helena, Marco, Walter, even Leo and Miriam.

And yet, through all of it, life goes on, ordinary and mysterious, revealing the future in random slivers — odd jigsaw pieces with no discernible pattern — as if the human eye were only capable of taking in the unknown one image at a time.

By the time Christophe is ready to leave, Nerina has convinced herself she wouldn't have it any other way.

Acknowledgements

Writing is a solitary occupation, but by the time a book reaches the final stages of publication, there are many people whose contributions merit acknowledgement.

I am grateful to Marc Côté for his steadfast support, his insightful editorial advice, and for often understanding my intentions better than I did, to Michael O'Leary for his keen eye and helpful suggestions, and to the other people at Cormorant Books who have left their mark on this book.

I am also grateful to Beverley Slopen for her discernment and encouragement, and to Ruth Portner for her patient and intelligent reading of every draft of this book.

I would like to thank friends in Venice, Upstate New York, Manhattan, and Montreal who shared with me their homes, their stories, and, in some instances, the affection for their dogs.

And, as always, I am deeply grateful for the support of family and friends, both near and distant; without them, writing and life do not bear imagining.